WHERE I BELONG

When a mysterious Italian man arrives on the doorstep in a storm, Maria can hardly turn him away, even though the guesthouse is closed for the winter. Maria's gentle care helps Dino recover from his distressing news, and soon she risks losing her heart to this charismatic stranger. But he has commitments that will take him far away, and her future is at the guesthouse. Can two people from different walks of life find a way to be together?

Books by Helen Scott Taylor
in the Linford Romance Library:

THE PERFECT HUSBAND

HELEN SCOTT TAYLOR

WHERE I BELONG

Complete and Unabridged

LINFORD
Leicester

First published in Great Britain in 2012

First Linford Edition
published 2013

A catalogue record for this book is available
from the British Library.

ISBN 978–1–4448–1579–5

Published by
F. A. Thorpe (Publishing)
Anstey, Leicestershire

Set by Words & Graphics Ltd.
Anstey, Leicestershire
Printed and bound in Great Britain by
T. J. International Ltd., Padstow, Cornwall

This book is printed on acid-free paper

1

Maria Gardener wiped her face on her sleeve and examined the wall she had just painted. She angled her head, trying to see if she had missed anywhere. It was only mid-afternoon, but the awful weather meant it was prematurely dark, and she'd had to turn on the light. The golden wheat colour glowed, fresh and clean. The greasy finger marks had gone and the guesthouse entrance hall would be ready to start next season spotless and welcoming.

Happy with her work, she pushed the lid onto the paint can, then bent and started gathering up the newspaper she'd spread to protect the Victorian mosaic floor. Her parents closed the place each winter and left for a month's cruise. For the last few years, she had used the quiet time to redecorate. This year she was making good progress.

They had only been gone for two days, and already she had finished a room.

Wind buffeted the front of the house, whistling through gaps in the casement windows while rain pelted against the glass. She almost wished she was with her mum and dad, boarding their cruise ship in Florida. Almost. Despite the weather, she would still rather be at home.

As she gathered up her paintbrushes the doorbell chimed. It couldn't be her sister, Chris; she'd be with her twins at playgroup. And, in this weather, none of the locals would be daft enough to walk up the hill to the Crow's Nest guesthouse on its rocky perch overlooking the village of Porthale. If any tourists were brave enough to visit Cornwall in winter, they would surely have seen the large CLOSED sign on the front gate. So who was her mystery caller?

Maria dropped her brushes onto the newspaper and stripped off her paint-stained gloves before unlocking the door. It swung against her in a gust of wet wind.

A dripping man stood on the top step huddled into his jacket. Maria stepped back and gestured him inside. Whoever he was, she couldn't leave him standing outside in the downpour.

Safely out of the rain, he ran his fingers back through gleaming black hair, scattering drips on the newspaper. Water trailed down his skin, caught in his thick black eyelashes. Foreign, she thought; Italian or Spanish, perhaps. She noticed a leather holdall in his hand and decided he must be looking for somewhere to stay. With the low light and bad weather he could have missed the closed sign, or his English might not be good.

'I'm very sorry,' she said clearly so that he would understand, 'we're cl — ' But her words died in her mouth as he turned his gaze on her.

He was beautiful; golden skin, classic good looks, but that wasn't what broke her train of thought. His bleak expression did that. Lines of tension bracketed his mouth and fanned out from deep brown eyes filled with anguish.

'Do you have a room?' he asked in soft, accented English.

She should say no, suggest he went to Truro where the hotels remained open all year, but instinct would not let her turn away someone in need.

Instead she nodded and went to the bureau they used as a reception desk. They had twelve bedrooms and during the winter shutdown, four underwent a makeover. She chose the key to room twelve, a family room at the far end of the upstairs corridor, the room furthest away from where she would be painting. She knew it was made up as she had checked it a week ago.

Opening the guest register, she glanced over her shoulder to find him staring into space.

'What is your name, please?'

He blinked and focused on her. 'Mr

Rossellini.' He spelled it out for her. 'It's Italian,' he added.

'How long do you plan to stay, Mr Rossellini?'

He shook his head slowly, the vacant expression sliding back into his eyes. 'I don't know.'

'No worries. You're the only guest so it doesn't matter.' She closed the bureau and headed towards the stairs. 'Follow me, please.' As Maria mounted the steps, she remembered she had a hole in the seat of her old leggings, and she was wearing one of her dad's ancient T-shirts, one that had once been black but was now a washed-out grey with 'Led Zeppelin' written across the front. And she probably had paint on her face. Not that Mr Rossellini was likely to notice. He seemed so preoccupied; she wondered if he even knew where he was.

He followed her along the hall to room twelve. She opened the door and led him inside. He pulled up with a sharp intake of breath and stared at the baby's cot.

'I hope you don't mind having a family room,' she said quickly. 'It has an ensuite bathroom and lovely sea views.'

Not that he would see much out of the windows right now. An American family who stayed last summer had called the outlook a 'million-dollar view', but at the moment the large bay window overlooking the harbour was awash with rain.

Gradually the Italian's tense shoulders eased, and he moved into the room. He wearily dropped his bag and wandered towards the window.

'Would you like me to put your leather jacket in the drying room, Mr Rossellini?' She glanced down at his expensive-looking black shoes. 'Your shoes as well, if you like.'

He didn't seem to hear her. She moved closer, her gaze sweeping from his broad shoulders to his narrow hips. He was rather gorgeous, and his clothes and bag looked expensive. He belonged in an upmarket city hotel, not a family-run guesthouse. Especially one that was supposed to be closed for the winter.

'Mr Rossellini,' she tried again, 'shall I dry your jacket?'

He didn't look at her, but he unbuttoned the jacket, slipped it off his shoulders and held it out.

'Will you be wanting dinner?'

He shook his head and resumed staring out through the rivulets of rain snaking down the glass.

'Okay. Well, come down if you want anything.' Maria hastened to the door and slipped out, closing it quietly. The poor man was hurting for some reason; that much was obvious. She hated seeing anyone unhappy. Her greatest joy was hearing the laughter of the families who stayed at the Crow's Nest. The bucket and spade brigade, her dad called them. Along with the hikers who stayed a night or two during a trek around the Cornish coast, families were the guesthouse's mainstay.

She made her way downstairs and went to the drying room beside the laundry at the back. Carefully she arranged the leather jacket on a hanger. It was certainly expensive, the leather and the satin lining both of good quality. She smoothed her hand down the wet sleeve, wishing she could smooth away the stranger's troubles.

While he was here, she would do her best to pull him out of his dismal mood, make him forget his worries and relax. Her dad joked that she always had to have a project. The decorating was her current one, but Mr Rossellini could be a small side project. She made herself a promise: by the time he left here she would have him laughing.

★   ★   ★

Maria was down in the kitchen by seven the next morning. She didn't expect her guest to be ready for breakfast this early, but according to Murphy's Law, he would come down at exactly the moment the carpet fitters arrived. So she wanted to have everything prepared.

First she fed Arthur, the village tom cat who turned up at her door every three or four days. He wolfed down his meat, then sauntered out again as though he owned the place.

In the dining room, Maria set the table in the bay window, the one with the nicest view, and put out the various breakfast cereals and fruit juices. She checked the contents of the fridge to make sure she had all the ingredients to cook a full English breakfast. Mr Rossellini was bound to be ravenous as he hadn't come down for dinner the previous night. When she was ready for him, she prepared herself some toast and coffee. Then she waited.

The kitchen was at the back of the house, but she had a view down the corridor past the office to the dining room. She leaned against the kitchen counter, sipping coffee and watching for the Italian. She tried to read a novel but couldn't concentrate. Every noise made her gaze jump from the page. Then water gushed down the pipe outside the back door, which, as Mr Rossellini was the only person upstairs, meant he must be showering.

Abandoning her book, she switched on the coffee machine and checked the kettle was full. Then she paced.

This was crazy. She and her mum and dad managed twelve rooms full of guests, but this one man had Maria in a spin.

The phone rang, and she was so wound up she nearly jumped out of her skin. She muttered a rude word under her breath and grabbed the handset.

As she started to answer, her sister Christine's voice cut in. 'Mari, can you do me a huge, huge favour and look after the girls for an hour this afternoon? Eric's hurt his back, and I need to take him to the chiropractor.'

Maria had intended to start decorating the upstairs rooms once the carpet fitters finished, but she had four weeks before her parents came home, so it wouldn't matter if she missed one afternoon. 'Okay. Hope Eric's all right.'

'You're a gem. I'll see you later.' Chris rang off.

Maria turned to look out of the window where a few streaks of blue sky had broken through the clouds, and decided that if the rain stayed away, she would take her nieces down to the beach. At that moment a door slammed. She pivoted around, wide-eyed. Typical! She looked away for a second and missed her guest. She dashed along the corridor to the front hall.

She'd left Mr Rossellini's leather jacket over the chair in the lobby. It had gone, but he wasn't in the dining room. She wrenched open the front door and raced out to the car park, just in time to see him striding away down the lane towards the village. Why hadn't he eaten breakfast? Perhaps he didn't know it was included in the room rate. But surely he would have asked? He'd missed two meals now. She watched his tall, lean form disappear round a corner and bit her lip.

Apart from worrying about him missing the meals, she was disappointed she hadn't managed to chat to him and find out how he was. She also wanted him to move his car, so that the carpet lorry had more room to turn. She wandered over to his sleek black BMW. A sticker in the window told her it was a hire car. Where had he come from? Surely not all the way from Italy.

Her breath hissed out in frustration and she returned to tidy up the kitchen. Now she wouldn't have a chance to ask him what he wanted for dinner tonight — if he wanted anything at all! Perhaps he didn't think the food in the guesthouse would be up to his standards. Catering for one guest was definitely more difficult than for a houseful.

Just in case he did deign to try her

cooking, she prepared boeuf bourgui-gnon and put it in the slow cooker while she waited for the carpet delivery. She also rang the wife of one of the local fishermen and asked if they could send up some of today's catch, so that her errant Italian had a choice of menu. Anything he didn't eat, she would freeze or eat herself.

At nine-thirty the carpet delivery van arrived and she watched as they hefted the huge rolls upstairs. All four of the bedrooms due for redecorating were off limits this morning. Two were being carpeted, and the other two were temporarily stuffed with the displaced furniture.

While the carpets were fitted, she gathered cleaning materials and went to service room twelve.

Visitors usually left belongings around their rooms, giving them a lived-in look. Mr Rossellini was either very tidy or he hadn't unpacked. She vacuumed, made the bed and restocked the tea and coffee tray, relieved to see he had at least made himself two cups of coffee and eaten the small complimentary packs of biscuits.

His leather holdall still looked wet. She prodded it with her toe. It was heavy. Full of damp, creased clothes that should be hung up, no doubt. She itched to take it down to the drying room, empty the bag, and dry and iron the lot, but that would be too presumptuous of her.

The black shoes he'd been wearing when he arrived were neatly placed under a chair and they, too, were damp. She grabbed them with a sigh and took them downstairs to dry. It wasn't much, but it went some way towards soothing her itch to take care of the man.

After lunch, her sister brought Charlotte and Poppy over, Maria's eighteen-month-old twin nieces. It had started to drizzle, so the beach was out. Instead, Maria made pastry and helped each of the girls to roll some out and make jam tarts, while she prepared a lemon meringue pie and some muffins.

Although she was busy, her thoughts

kept slipping back to her Italian guest, wondering where he was, what he was doing, if he was all right. The misery in his eyes the previous night haunted her. She hated to see anyone so unhappy.

By six, she was on edge, listening for the front door. Mr Rossellini had been gone for nine hours. If he'd taken his car, she wouldn't have worried, but he'd walked — and he was not dressed for hiking.

* * *

Dino Rossellini sat on a rocky outcrop overlooking the Cornish fishing village and stared at the bright specks of light in the darkness that pinpointed ships far out to sea. When he was a boy, the sound of waves beating against rocks had energised him, excited him. Now it did nothing to rouse him from his desolate, dark mood.

His feet were wet and cold. A bitter chill hardened inside him, but the feeling was only partly due to the cool

15

of the night. He had tramped along the deserted coast paths for hours in an effort to walk away his hollow feeling of grief. It had not worked. His mind had endlessly replayed his conversation with his ex, Rachel. How his joy at learning he had a baby son had turned to despair when she told him that she had given his child away.

He'd got straight on the phone to the adoption agency, but no matter how hard he'd argued and pleaded, they said he could not see his son. Although he'd had no say in the matter, his baby boy now belonged to someone else! How did British law allow such a thing? Pain, anger and frustration raged through him anew, and he hurled a rock down into the dark waters below. This was all the fault of Dino's snake of a manager, Freddy Short. Apparently, he had encouraged Rachel not to tell Dino about the pregnancy. He'd claimed to be protecting Dino's career, but what he'd really been protecting was his own percentage.

Overcome by the injustice and betrayal, Dino had walked out of Freddy's office, rented a car and headed out of London; just driven, with no idea where he was going. When the car ran low on petrol, he'd stopped in Truro to refuel and seen a photo of the fishing village of Porthale. It reminded him of the place where he grew up. A place where family was still valued; where people lived simple, wholesome lives. A place off the beaten track where he might not be recognised.

At the thought of home, he pulled his phone from his pocket and for the first time since he walked out after his argument with Freddy, he switched it on. Immediately it chimed to notify him of emails, texts and voice messages. Ignoring them, he dialled his parents' number in Italy.

'Si?' His mother answered.

'It's Dino, Mamma,' he said in Italian.

'Dino, Dino, where are you? Freddy

Short rang us to find out if you were here.'

'I'm sorry if he worried you, Mamma. I'm okay. I just need some time on my own.'

'It is a relief to hear your voice, chicco. We see so little of you these days. We miss you.'

'I miss you, too. I know I haven't been home for ages, but I promise I will be there for your birthday. I must go now. Ciao, Mamma. Ciao.'

He gripped the phone to his chest after he finished the call, tears in his eyes. He hadn't been able to see his family at Christmas this year because Freddy had booked him solid over the holiday season. He had intended to visit them during this rare break in his schedule, but he couldn't go home feeling like this. His mamma would take one look at him and know something was badly wrong.

He wished he could tell her he had a son, but he could never share this secret with his parents. It would break their hearts to hear they had a grandson, only to learn they could never see him. He could not even share this tragedy with his best friend Romeo, as he would not understand. He must bear this grief alone. With a shiver he got to his feet, hands deep in his jacket pockets, and walked towards the village.

⋆ ⋆ ⋆

It was nearly dark when Maria finally heard the front door. She darted along the corridor to the entrance hall and caught the Italian with his foot on the bottom stair.

'Mr Rossellini,' she gasped, breathlessly, and blushed when he frowned at her. He must think she'd been lying in wait to pounce on him — and she had.

'You didn't have breakfast. It's included in the room rate.'

He shrugged. 'No matter.'

'Do you want dinner? I won't charge you for it to make up for the breakfast you missed.' She cringed. That wasn't what she'd planned to say. It sounded as though she was trying to bribe him to eat her food.

He moved his hand in a careless gesture of acceptance.

'I will have dinner, please.'

Relief burst through her, which was crazy. He was a strapping six foot of healthy male. He wasn't about to fade away from lack of a meal or two.

'I only have two choices, I'm afraid. Are you happy with boeuf bourguignon, or would you like sea bass?'

He sniffed the air. 'If that is the beef I smell, then it will be acceptable.'

As he continued up the stairs, she quickly added, 'Eight o'clock, then?'

He turned, lean hand gripping the handrail, and glanced down at her. 'Eight it is.'

She watched him mount the rest of the stairs and noticed he was barefoot. A muddy pair of what must have once been smart suede shoes, stuffed with wet socks, sat beside the front door in the plastic tray intended for dirty walking boots. She grabbed them and deposited them in the drying room to tend to later.

With renewed purpose, Maria returned to the kitchen and baked some dinner rolls with dough she had prepared earlier. Then she made a crème brûlée and put it in the fridge, hoping it would chill in time to serve that night. Just before eight o'clock, she changed the breakfast table setting for dinner, lit a candle, and placed a wine list on the table. She slotted an easy-listening music CD into the player and turned it on softly. Then she lowered the lights and stood back to gauge the effect. The soft music, candle and low lighting felt too romantic, so she turned the lights back up in case her guest got the wrong idea.

At five to eight, Mr Rossellini came into the dining room. He'd changed into a black shirt and a slightly wrinkled emerald cashmere sweater.

'Good evening,' he said, and a tingle

raced down her spine. It was strange how English sounded so much sexier when spoken in an Italian accent.

'Good evening, Mr Rossellini. Please sit down.' She indicated the table by the window. The weather had cleared, giving a beautiful view of the village below. Tiny points of light from the cottage windows trailed down the hill and clustered around the harbour like a garland of fairy lights. 'Would you like a starter? I have spicy cucumber soup or scallops.'

'No, thank you.' He broke open one of the warm bread rolls. 'You baked this?' he asked, a hint of surprise in his voice.

'Yes. Cooking is one of my passions.'

He took a bite and nodded his approval. 'Very good . . . What is your name, please?'

'Maria.'

'Very good, Maria.' Her name rolled off his tongue with the honeyed inflection of an endearment and her cheeks heated. Although she was sure he hadn't meant anything by it. In his accent, the word 'toilet' probably sounded sexy!

'I'll fetch your boeuf bourguignon.' She hurried towards the kitchen, her pulse racing, and carefully dished out the beef with dauphinoise potatoes, green beans and baby carrots. Then she carried his steaming plate through to him. He had seemed brighter than yesterday, but as she re-entered the dining room, she found him staring blankly into space, his lips tight, his half-eaten roll forgotten on his side plate. Her heart dropped. Whatever was troubling him was still very much on his mind.

He sucked in a breath as she approached and moved his hands so she could put down his plate. He gave her a perfunctory smile. 'Thank you. This looks delicious.'

'Can I get you anything else? A bottle of wine, perhaps?'

He shook his head and indicated his glass of water.

'This is good.'

It was on the tip of her tongue to ask whether he was all right, but that would be stupid as he obviously wasn't. She really wanted to ask what was troubling him. If she knew, she might be able to help. The words nearly burst from her mouth, but she managed to bite them back. She shouldn't pry. His problems were none of her business.

Instead, she reluctantly headed back to the kitchen, ladled out a helping of beef for herself, and then sat at the kitchen table to eat. She opened her book and read a few pages, but she couldn't concentrate.

'Rossellini,' she whispered to herself, rolling the word over her tongue in a fake Italian accent. 'Maria Rossellini.'

That sounded good. She had the crazy urge to write it down like a besotted teenager. But she wasn't besotted; she just found him fascinating and mysterious.

When she had finished eating, she went back to the dining room, keen to

24

see if he wanted the crème brûlée or
lemon meringue pie for dessert. Disappointment kicked in her chest at the
sight of his empty chair. He must have
crept out, or she'd have heard him. But
his plate was clean, so at least he'd
eaten a decent meal. Her goal for
Wednesday was to get him to eat
breakfast as well — even if she had to
stake out the entrance hall in the
morning to stop him escaping.

2

Wednesday started well. The sun was shining and Maria's Italian guest ate a full English breakfast before he disappeared out of the front door.

As soon as he left, she hot-footed it upstairs to clean his room before she went out. She entered number twelve and with a guilty little murmur of pleasure, inhaled the delicious spicy smell of his aftershave. She paused during her cleaning to enjoy the glorious view from the window and noticed a lone figure that looked like Mr Rossellini, striding along the coast path to the south of the village. She squinted against the sunlight and watched as he halted on the Jacka, the huge rocky outcrop that towered over the harbour.

While he stared out to sea, she stared at him. What was he thinking? What kept him out alone all day?

She had tried to make small talk at breakfast, to find out where he'd gone the previous day, but all he'd answered was that he'd walked the coast path.

With a glance at her watch she tore herself away from the window, hurried downstairs and prepared to go out.

After she locked up, she walked down the lane to the village. The ancient slate-roofed cottages crowded along the narrow street, a mix of grey stone and whitewashed walls, a few hardy flowers in hanging baskets and the shop signs providing bright splashes of colour.

The committee running the annual fundraiser for the local playgroup was meeting in the Plume of Feathers, the pub by the harbour, and she was one of the eight committee members. She pushed open the pub door and walked through the rustic splendour of the oak-panelled bar with its many brass knick-knacks, to the airy modern conservatory that served as a restaurant. Amid a veritable jungle of pot plants and hanging flowers, most of her fellow committee members were already seated around a pine dining table, chatting and drinking coffee.

'Morning, Maria! Ready for action?' Philip, the owner of the pub, rubbed his hands together. He was new to the pub trade and the village. An ex-Royal Marine, he seemed to have boundless energy and infected everyone with his enthusiasm. His wife Millie sat at his side, joggling their two-year-old daughter on her knee, making the little girl giggle.

Maria wasn't surprised to find that her sister, Chris, hadn't arrived yet. Punctuality had never been her forte. After Maria had said her hellos, she took a seat.

'Want a coffee?' Philip held up a cafetiére. She nodded and as he poured, Chris burst in with a bulky bag over her shoulder, towing a small golden-haired daughter by each hand.

Maria jumped up and took Charlotte from her. 'Hello, munchkin, how are you this morning?' She sat the toddler on her lap and kissed her golden curls.

'They're grumpy,' Chris said, dumping her bag beside a chair and sitting with her other daughter, Poppy, on her lap. 'Charlie's teething and it's disturbing Poppy's sleep.'

'Oh, poor baby.' Maria hugged Charlotte tighter, breathing her lovely baby smell. One day, she wanted her own little girl, and she couldn't wait. It wasn't fashionable nowadays for young women to want homes and babies; they all wanted careers, but Maria longed for nothing more than a husband and children to care for. Her mother said she belonged in a bygone era.

'Shall we get started? It doesn't look as though the other two are going to show,' Philip said, a hint of censure in his voice.

'Blast,' Chris interrupted as Philip started to talk about catering. 'I've left the girl's toy bag in the car.'

'Don't worry.' Maria dug in her handbag and pulled out two crayons.

She tore in half the paper she had brought to take notes and gave a piece and a crayon to each of her nieces.

'You're a gem,' Chris said gratefully.

'That's what aunties are for, isn't it, precious?' she said, smiling at Poppy.

As Philip updated them on the budget, Maria watched Charlotte scribble red lines on the paper, wishing she had her own daughter on her lap. But first she needed a husband, and she wasn't having much luck on that front.

Tom had been her last serious boyfriend, but that ended three years ago. They'd met a few weeks after she started at university and been together the whole time. She'd thought he was The One, but everything changed when they finished uni. He wanted to travel, to see the world before he settled down.

Against her better judgment, she'd let him persuade her to go with him to Canada and work as a chalet girl, while he was a ski instructor for six months. Her degree was in hospitality management, and he'd said the experience would look good on her CV.

She had hated every moment. The people who stayed in the chalet partied, drank and stayed up all night. They had no consideration for anyone else, and the mess they created was unbelievable. The worst thing was that Tom fitted right in with them. She'd stuck it out for three months, then come home and pledged never to try anything like that again.

Her parents had encouraged her to get a job in a prestigious hotel, but she didn't want to work in a place where the guests were numbers on a computer screen and the smiles false. She had learned her lesson. She belonged at the Crow's Nest where the guests became friends.

'Maria?' Philip asked and she jolted back to the meeting.

'Sorry, what did you say?'

'Richard's let us down with the music. All he had to do was compile a playlist and burn the tracks to a CD, but he hasn't done it. You'll have time to sort out the music, won't you?'

'Oh.' She hesitated. She had no idea how to 'burn' a CD, but it should be easy enough to come up with a list of Fifties and Sixties songs for the 'hop' they were organising, and somebody could help her with the CD part.

'Okay. I'm sure I can do that.'

Philip grinned around the table and rubbed his hands together. 'Things are looking good, ladies and gents. Chris says we've already sold half the tickets. We're on target for a full house!' He glanced down at his notes one last time. 'That's us done for this week, folks. See you next week, then — same time, same place.'

Maria glanced at her sister, feeling guilty she had zoned out and missed Chris's report on ticket sales, but she knew her sister and brother-in-law Eric would sell lots of tickets; they seemed to know everyone.

Charlotte turned her cute little smile on Maria and she grinned back. 'Are you feeling better now, poppet?'

Charlotte pointed at her mouth and screwed up her nose. 'Tooths sore.'

'I need to get these two little rascals home and give them some lunch,' Chris said, hooking her bag over her shoulder and lifting Poppy onto a hip. Maria gathered her things and followed Chris out, giving Charlotte a cuddle before they said goodbye.

As they emerged into the car park, Chris halted at her car, staring towards the shingle beach. 'Wow, hottie alert!'

Maria followed her gaze to see Mr Rossellini chatting with Mark Trevarthan, one of the local fishermen who kept his boat in the harbour. Her Italian guest was wearing sunglasses, the sun gleaming off his luxuriant black hair and her heart gave a little jump at the sight of him. He had seemed reluctant to talk at breakfast, but he looked happier now, conversing easily with Mark. As she watched them, the two men clambered up on the deck of the green, wooden fishing boat and examined a crab pot. Mr Rossellini gestured freely as they chatted, lithe and animated, he exuded energy and charisma.

Maria hadn't noticed it so much in the guesthouse, but out here, surrounded by the ordinary people from the village, the Italian seemed exotic and beautiful.

'I wonder what Mr Eye Candy is doing in Porthale.' Chris frowned. 'He looks vaguely familiar. Do you think he's an actor shooting a film in the area?' She glanced around. 'I can't see a sports car complete with the prerequisite glamorous blonde. Perhaps he's on his own.'

Maria tried to keep her expression neutral. It occurred to her that having a man stay at the guesthouse while she was there alone did not look good. Perhaps she should have thought it through more carefully before she offered him a room.

Chris nudged Maria's arm. 'You should go and chat him up. If he's still around in three weeks, he'd be one hot date for the hop.' Chris grinned, but her eyes narrowed as she studied Maria; she knew that look on her sister's face. 'You know who he is, don't you, Sis? Come on — you have to spill the beans!'

'He's staying in the Crow's Nest for a few days,' Maria admitted rather sheepishly.

'Him?' Chris's eyes opened like saucers, and she gazed at him some more. 'What's a man like that doing staying at the Nest? Hey!' She swung back to Maria. 'The place is meant to be closed.' Then a slow smile spread across her face. 'You bad, bad girl. Don't tell me he's your — '

'Gracious, no!' Maria replied before Chris's imagination soared completely out of control. 'Where would I have met a man like that? He just appeared on the doorstep on Monday night. I couldn't turn him away in that deluge, could I now?'

'Of course not.' Chris gave her a conspiratorial smile. 'A woman would have to be brain-dead to send him packing.' Having strapped Poppy into her car seat, she walked round to repeat the process with Charlotte.

Eager to change the subject, Maria turned the conversation to more mundane matters. 'I've made a good start on the decorating. If Eric's back's bad, I suppose he won't be fit enough to help me move the furniture back in, now that the carpet guys have been?'

Chris shook her head as she climbed into the driver's seat of her four-wheel drive. She lowered her window so they could continue to talk.

'Not for a few weeks. The chiropractor wants him to keep moving, but to take things easy. Maybe your Italian stallion can flex those gorgeous muscles and give you a hand.'

Maria bit her lip as she glanced back at Mr Rossellini. It would be really useful if he could help. Normally she wouldn't dream of asking a guest to move furniture, but the situation was not quite normal, and doing something constructive might help distract him from whatever was on his mind.

As she watched him, he noticed her and raised a hand.

'Maria, I have bought a crab,' he called. He swung down from the boat with the crab in a plastic bag and started across the shingle towards her. His blue shirt was open at the throat and his leather jacket was slung over his shoulder.

Little tingles raced through her, setting her heart fluttering. Gosh, he really was gorgeous. She might have taken on more than she'd bargained for when she agreed to let him stay.

* * *

The young woman who ran the guesthouse blushed as Dino walked up to her. Her long brown hair was tied back in a simple ponytail, and she was fresh-faced, only a touch of make-up on her skin. She wore jeans and a yellow blouse fastened with tiny pearly buttons shaped like flowers. He'd barely noticed her when he arrived, but she was pretty in an understated way — and she cooked like an angel; the boeuf bourguignon she had prepared had been delicious. His mother would approve of her.

'You are walking back now?' he gestured up the hill towards the guesthouse.

'Yes.' She flapped around with her bag and a sweater in her hand, looking flustered. She certainly wasn't like the women who pursued him so relentlessly that he needed bodyguards to escort him in and out of venues where he performed. As she started walking, he fell into step beside her.

'You're not staying out all day today, then?' she asked.

'The sun is shining. I would like to sit in your garden if that is acceptable.'

'Of course. The weather is weird this winter. It almost feels like spring today.' She glanced away, and then cast him a shy sideways glance. 'Would you like me to cook you lunch?'

He smiled, despite the deep melancholy that still weighed down his heart. She was as eager to feed him as his mother always was. 'Do you think I am too thin?'

'Gosh, no. I'm just worried that you missed two meals in a row, and you were out for so long yesterday, using up energy.'

Why would a complete stranger worry about him? He had stayed in the best hotels money could buy, all over the world. The staff he met were mostly polite, but none of them cared whether he chose to eat or not.

As they reached the top of the street and turned up the lane to the guesthouse, she pointed at the bag containing his purchase. 'You like crab, then?'

'My father and two of my brothers are fishermen. It was good to talk of things that remind me of home. I bought the crab to show my gratitude.' Discussing tides, the catch, and the unpredictable weather had taken him back to a simpler time; a time when he'd helped his father at weekends for pocket money.

'You obviously didn't join the family business,' she observed.

'Ah, Maria, you are right,' he said wistfully. They had reached the guest-house gate. He opened it and stared out to sea as the young woman passed him, wondering, not for the first time, if his life might have been happier if he had stayed in Riomaggiore, married a local girl and lived the simple life of a fisherman. But singing was his passion, always had been, and his spirit would wither if he could not sing for people. He could never give it up, not for anyone or anything.

★ ★ ★

While Mr Rossellini went into the garden, Maria defrosted and cooked some part-baked rolls and a portion of home-made mushroom soup. When the lunch was ready, she carried it out on a tray with a napkin and cutlery.

She paused beneath the arched trellis leading into the sheltered walled garden beside the Crow's Nest. In the unseasonably warm weather, her Italian was enjoying the suntrap. Head tipped back and eyes closed, he was listening to something through earphones attached to his mobile phone. She admired him for a moment, then went forward.

'I've brought your lunch.' She raised her voice so he would hear over his music. His thick black lashes lifted and the weight of his gaze rested on her. He'd appeared distracted up until then, lost in the turmoil of his thoughts. Now when his languorous, brown eyes settled on her, she felt the intensity of his presence like a physical touch.

He pulled the earphones from his ears, and faint strains of classical music sounded for a moment before he switched it off.

'Thank you, Maria.' He straightened and examined his bowl.

'It's my homemade mushroom soup.'

She winced inside at her eager tone. She must stop blowing her own trumpet.

He unfolded the napkin she had wrapped around the warm rolls and the corners of his lips twitched. 'This is perfect, Maria.' His gaze rose to her again. For a moment she couldn't breathe, then heat rushed to her cheeks.

'I'm going upstairs for a while. When I come down, I'll make you a cup of coffee.' She hurried upstairs intent on doing something useful and not thinking about Mr Rossellini.

* * *

Dino tasted the soup and his eyes closed with pleasure. Sublime; she was a culinary angel. He glanced at the upstairs windows thoughtfully. In his home village of Riomaggiore, a pretty young woman who cooked as well as Maria would have suitors lining up at her door. Granted, Dino had not been paying attention up until now, but

Maria wore no rings and he had not noticed a boyfriend visiting. The men in Porthale must be blind and stupid not to have snapped her up.

He had just finished his soup and picked up his napkin when a blood-curdling scream rang out from upstairs. Dino leaped out of his chair and tossed his napkin down. Had she fallen from a ladder, or cut herself perhaps? He raced inside, bounded up the stairs three at a time, and slid to a halt outside the open door of a bedroom.

Maria was inside, huddled in the far corner by the window. The healthy pink roses that had earlier coloured her cheeks were gone, her complexion now chalk-white. Dino glanced around the room at a loss to see anything out of place.

'What is the matter?'

She gnawed her lips, staring at a heap of plastic sheet on the ground in front of her. 'It's in there.' Her gaze flicked up to him then back to the plastic. 'A spider — a really massive one!'

The tension in Dino's shoulders drained away 'Ah, cara, cara . . . ' He shook his head, suppressed a smile, strolled in and nudged the folded plastic with his toe. A spider scuttled out.

Maria's scream rent the air again and Dino winced; she definitely did not have a singing career in her future, but she probably had a sore throat coming.

The spider had secreted itself beneath another fold and was hidden once more. 'Let me take this out for you,' he offered.

'Yes! Yes, please.'

He caught hold of the corners and gathered the plastic sheet into a bundle, then carried it downstairs. He heard Maria's footsteps behind him on the stairs. He went out of the front door to the car park and flapped the sheet.

'Where did it go? It won't get back in the house, will it?' she asked from the safety of the front step.

He hadn't seen the spider fall out, but this called for a white lie. If she thought it might still be inside, his culinary angel would probably shut herself in her room, and he wouldn't get any dinner. 'It is in the hedge, Maria.'

'Oh.' She ventured a short way down the front path and peered at the hedge as if it might bite her.

Dino bundled the sheet up again and headed inside. 'Come, cara. I will spread this out for you to put your mind at rest.'

* * *

Maria hurried after the Italian, feeling like a complete twit. What would he think of her now? But at least he seemed happier. If rescuing her from her silly phobia took his mind off his worries, then some good had come of it.

When they got back to room one, he spread the sheet on the floor, then repeated the process with the other four small plastic sheets while Maria watched tensely from the doorway, ready to bolt if another eight-legged fiend appeared.

'There you are.' He dusted his hands together.

'I know it's silly being afraid of spiders when we don't have poisonous ones here, but their legs are just . . . ' She shivered.

He shrugged. 'Do not worry about it. My brother is this tall.' He held his hand a few inches above his head. 'He is terrified of spiders. And my mamma, who is this tall — ' He bumped the edge of his hand half way down his chest. 'She has to carry them outside for him.'

He was trying to make her feel better about her phobia. Sweet of him, considering she had disturbed his lunch. 'Let me make you a coffee, Mr Rossellini. I think you've earned it.'

'Now I know your shameful secret, I think you should call me Dino.' He leaned on the door frame, watching her.

Dino. That was cute, and suited him. She looked down to hide her smile.

'Okay, Dino it is then.' It wasn't unusual for her to call guests by their first names. They didn't stand on ceremony at the Crow's Nest. So why did this feel different?

★ ★ ★

A few days later, Maria sat on the floor in the sitting room, a heap of CDs beside her along with a pen and pad. She was babysitting Poppy and Charlotte, who were both playing happily on the carpet nearby, Poppy quietly fitting shapes into holes and Charlotte noisily thumping the keys of her small plastic organ.

Maria turned over a CD that her dad played in the dining room and squinted at the song titles, looking for dates. Did anything on here qualify as suitable for the playgroup hop? She really was hopeless with music. She had no idea what people had listened to in the Fifties and Sixties.

She released a frustrated sigh. A hop

needed dance music, and that wasn't something her family listened to. That meant she would have to search through someone else's music collection, or try to find songs on the internet. She should have asked Philip to give this job to someone else. She needed to learn to say no sometimes.

Movement out of the corner of her eye made her look up. Dino stood in the open doorway, a hand rested on either side of the door frame and a frown on his face.

'Good afternoon, Maria. These are your daughters?'

'My what? Oh, no!' Her hand rose to her heart at the thought. If only they were. 'They're my nieces.'

'Ah!' His expression cleared and he ambled into the room. 'They have a resemblance to you.'

'Do they?' Maria had never noticed that the girls looked like her, but then she hadn't thought about it before.

As Dino came into the room, Poppy moved closer to Maria and cuddled against her arm, while extrovert Charlotte banged her organ even more loudly and started shouting, showing off.

'You have a musician in the family,' Dino observed with a smile of wry humour.

Maria grinned as Charlotte clambered to her feet and toddled across to Dino before presenting him with the organ. 'Dance, dance,' she shouted.

He took the offered toy and shot Maria a questioning glance. 'She wants me to dance?'

'No. She wants you to play so *she* can dance.'

He smiled at the little girl and perched on the edge of an armchair, the organ across his knees. Then he started to play. Maria expected the usual random assortment of notes she was used to hearing as none of her family could play. Instead, real music came out of the organ. Charlotte jumped around, waving her arms. After a few minutes, Poppy couldn't resist

49

joining her. Dino continued playing catchy tunes that segued seamlessly from one to another.

'You can actually play real music on it!' She laughed at the girls' antics.

'Hmmm.' Dino pulled a face. 'Maria, not even a maestro would be able to play real music on this toy.'

'Well it sounds like music to me.'

Finally Charlotte got over-excited and started banging the organ along with Dino, creating the familiar ear-splitting racket. Poppy started to cry.

'Okay, you two. That's enough.' Maria rose and Dino handed her the organ. She hid it behind a big pot on the mantelpiece. 'Time for a drink and a nap, I think.'

She lifted both girls onto the sofa and handed them their cups. They started drinking their milk and sleepy eyelids fell.

Dino nodded towards the CDs strewn across the floor. 'You are searching for something?'

She flopped into a chair and poked at

the plastic cases with her toe. 'I have to assemble a playlist for a Sixties hop we're running as a playgroup fund-raiser. I'm not having much luck.'

Dino went down on his knees and sorted through the music discs, then threw up his hands with a sound of displeasure.

'You have terrible taste!'

She stared at him a little taken aback by his bluntness. Then she laughed. 'You're an expert, I suppose?'

'I most certainly am.' He slouched back against the armchair he'd vacated, all dark and brooding and thoughtful. Her heart did strange little leaps and bounds as she watched him.

'I suggest *Dirty Dancing*,' he offered.

'Dirty what? Oh, you mean the film!' That was actually a really good idea. If she could find a film soundtrack or compilation of suitable songs, she wouldn't need to burn any music to CD. And she knew exactly who to ask; her sister's neighbour, Tina, loved movie soundtracks.

'Great idea. You've just earned your dinner.'

Charlotte and Poppy had both fallen asleep drinking their milk. Maria set their cups on a table and tucked a blanket over them, making sure they wouldn't roll off the sofa.

'Watch the girls for a moment, will you, please?'

She dashed through to the kitchen and quickly phoned Chris to ask her to bring the *Dirty Dancing* CD over when she picked up her daughters. Then she made Dino a cup of tea, put a home-made double chocolate muffin on a plate and hurried back to the sitting room.

He had settled in a chair and was leafing through one of the children's plastic books. As she walked in, the book mooed, and he grinned like a little boy. He quickly set it aside when she handed him the tea.

'So, you are going to the hop in old-fashioned clothes?' he asked her.

She wouldn't call her outfit old-fashioned exactly, but she knew what he

52

meant. 'Yes, I've got something suitable for the era. I just have to learn how to dance now,' she joked. Although she didn't really intend to bother. She wouldn't be dancing much, anyway.

'Let me teach you.'

'To what — dance?'

'Salsa.' He rose and danced across the room with the athletic grace of a man who knew exactly how to move.

Watching him shimmy, the fluid movements of his body, Maria forgot to breathe.

He approached, hands extended. 'Come, Maria, it is simple. We will start with the five basic steps, forwards and back.'

'Gosh. I don't know . . . ' She was quite likely to end up a puddle of mush at his feet, but he was there in front of her, hands outstretched, demanding a response. She couldn't just ignore him. 'Oh, all right. I'll give it a try.'

With a tingle of nerves, she slipped her fingers into his and he pulled her closer. 'Now, cara, watch me.' He counted as he stepped forwards and back. 'Your turn.'

Maria felt her cheeks heat as she copied his steps, but rather less elegantly.

'Again,' he said. She made another attempt and he repeated his command.

'You're taking this very seriously.'

'Ay ay ay, Maria. Do you not know that you must practise if you are to learn?' He took one of her hands.

She glanced up from her feet to his intense expression. This was a new side of him, this concentration and focus. She got the feeling he probably gave everything he did one hundred and ten percent. Whatever his job, he must be good at it. She was willing to bet that nothing short of excellence would satisfy him.

She practised a few more times, then he took both her hands and began to dance with her.

At first she watched her feet, but that was difficult when they were dancing together. She raised her gaze to find him watching her, a smile playing at the corners of his mouth.

'You see, Maria,' he said, drawing her name out in a long, sexy drawl. 'You can do it if you want to.'

He showed her another move, a turn, and held her hand above her head as she twirled. His fingers were warm on hers and as she looked into the rich brown of his eyes, she realised that she liked this man, really liked him. She was in danger of falling for him; in fact, she admitted, she was already half way down that slippery slope.

But if she lost her heart to Dino Rossellini, she was setting herself up for disappointment. Even if he returned her feelings, a man such as he would never want to make his home at the Crow's Nest.

3

Later that day, as Maria prepared the dinner, her eye was drawn to the *Dirty Dancing* CD Chris had brought her. Maria had left the disc on the windowsill beside the small player, waiting for Dino to go out before she listened to it. If he caught her playing music, he would have her dancing again.

It wasn't that she didn't want to dance with him — quite the opposite. In every quiet moment since, she remembered the feel of his strong hands holding hers, the elegant way he moved. And that was exactly why she shouldn't dance with him again.

The effect he had on her was confusing, blurring the boundary between guest and friend. She needed to draw a line in the sand, keep him on one side and her on the other.

Already, she knew that she would miss him when he left, far more than she should.

She donned oven gloves and fetched the lasagne she'd prepared. Serving lasagne to Dino, who must be used to the genuine Italian version, was a risk but the dish was a favourite among their guests, so she had her fingers crossed that Dino would approve.

She placed the small ceramic bowl on a plate and while the pasta cooled, prepared a mixed salad, then she wrapped two warm rolls in a linen napkin and nestled them in a basket.

At eight on the dot, his tread sounded on the stairs. She poured a glass of chilled water from the refrigerator, added it to the tray, then went into the dining room. Usually he was seated and waiting, but tonight he stood at the bay window, his back to the room. The stiff set of his shoulders alerted her that something was wrong. As she entered and placed the tray on the table he pivoted around.

'Is everything all right, Dino?'

'This is not right.' He gestured at the food and Maria's heart dropped. She should have known not to serve the British version of Lasagne to an Italian.

'I'm sorry. This is one of our most popular dishes.' She hastened to remove it, racking her brain for another dish she could prepare quickly.

'No, no, I do not mean the food. It is not right that I should eat here alone while you do the same in the kitchen. Good food should be shared. Mealtimes are for relaxation and talk, a time to savour and enjoy. You will please join me for dinner tonight?'

Maria's heart fluttered like a trapped bird and her hand went to her chest. His invitation simply meant that he wanted company. Yet she felt as though she was slipping, falling, her emotions out of her control.

She glanced around the dining room at the other eleven polished wooden tables, the Victorian tiled fireplace on the far wall resplendent with a huge display of dried flowers in the hearth. She had lived at the Crow's Nest all her life, but she could count on her fingers the number of times she had eaten in the dining room.

Then she looked back at Dino. He had moved to the chair opposite his and pulled it out, encouraging her to sit down. 'It will be good to share the meal.' He smiled.

Common sense told her to decline, but there really was no way to turn down his request without being rude and hurtful.

She gave a hesitant smile. 'Okay, then. Let me just go and fetch my plate.'

She hurried back to the kitchen and stood for a moment, gripping the edge of the sink, wondering how her wish to help a stranger in distress had become so complicated. Her mum and dad would throw a wobbly if they knew she was here alone with a man she knew nothing about; a man who seemed to be taking control of how things were run.

With a fortifying breath, she placed her lasagne dish, salad and roll on a tray and carried it to the dining room. She half expected to find he had started eating, but he was standing where she'd left him, his hand on the back of her chair. She laid herself a place, and as she sat, he pushed the chair in for her. Only then did he take his seat with a smile of satisfaction.

'You see,' he gave an expansive gesture, 'this is much more pleasant. Now we can eat and talk and enjoy this lovely evening.' He tasted his lasagne and closed his eyes. 'This is delicious, wonderful, sublime. You are a culinary angel, cara. You have a magical touch.'

Maria looked down at her plate, her cheeks heating. She was used to guests thanking her for a nice meal, but she wasn't used to such extravagant compliments.

Looking at Dino's animated expression and sparkling eyes, she could hardly recall the morose, miserable man who had turned up on her door step a week ago. Delighted as she was to see his spirits restored, this vibrant, charismatic man also made her nervous.

'You like walking?' she asked, fumbling for something to say.

'Yes, I walk. A lot,' he added with a wry smile. 'I walk to think, to plan, to dispel anger and frustration, to enjoy the beautiful countryside, for the pleasure of being alive.'

'You don't find it too hilly along the coast here?'

'Your hills are nothing to me, cara. Where I come from, the hills are like this.' He angled his palm vertically.

'So where is that?' Maria asked, suddenly glad she'd joined him for dinner if it meant she could find out more about him.

'Have you heard of the Cinque Terre, the five lands?' When she shook her head he continued. 'These are five small towns on the Italian Riviera. It is rocky, very steep. My family, they live in Riomaggiore. Very beautiful, but full of tourists. When I was a boy, there were not so many and it was quiet, but now . . . ' He gave a dismissive gesture and sighed.

'Is it anything like Porthale?'

'Yes and no. Here, I show you.' He fished his phone from his pocket and switched it on. It chimed to alert him to messages, but he ignored them and scrolled through his pictures. 'Here, Maria, this is Riomaggiore.'

She took the offered phone and examined the screen. The village was like something out of a fairytale. Narrow, multicoloured houses, three and four storeys tall, were stacked up the cliffs like children's building blocks. Brightly coloured fishing boats drawn up on the shingle around the harbour resembled fish laid out to dry. Above the village, what looked like rows of grape vines patterned the terraced fields.

'Wow! This is so pretty. How could you bear to leave it?'

He shrugged and gestured in a way she was coming to recognise meant he didn't want to answer that question.

'So your family still lives here?'

'My father and two of my brothers are fishermen, as I told you, and my eldest brother, he has a fish restaurant. One of my sisters is at university in Rome and the other is married to a fisherman from Manarola, the next town along the coast.'

'That's convenient.'

He smiled. 'That is how things are there. People are good at providing for themselves. For years the area was cut off from the rest of Italy by mountains. Only recently was a road built.'

His warm tone of voice betrayed his affection for the place. 'You obviously love it.'

'I try to return when I can.'

'So what took you away from home?'

'I have to travel a lot,' he said, glancing away. She noticed he avoided answering the question, and although she wanted to know more about him, she let it go.

'And before you came here to

Cornwall, were you in London?' she asked, changing the subject.

'Ah, London.' Dino pulled a face. 'London is like Roma, too many people. Always people running everywhere like little ants. I needed a quiet place to think. So I came here.' He gestured again, taking in the village and the guesthouse.

She itched to ask him what he'd needed to think about, but she shouldn't pry. She forked in a mouthful of lasagne to help stifle the urge to ask. He had gone quiet now, looking down at his plate as he ate, obviously remembering what it was that had brought him here. She wished their conversation had not gone in this direction. She hated to see him subdued. He was so vital when he was happy, more alive than anyone else she knew.

'So you, Maria, why are you here in this place? Do you not have college or university to attend?'

'Been there, done that, got the

T-shirt,' she replied.

He frowned. 'A T-shirt?'

She smiled at his bemused expression. 'I have been to university, Dino. I studied hospitality management.'

'Yes, that is right for you, I think, but why are you not the manager of a big hotel by now?' he asked genuinely.

'I don't like cities full of people either. I like looking after the families with children who stay at the guest-house. We are one big, happy family here. A soulless big hotel is not for me.'

Their eyes met, and a moment of understanding passed between them that stroked across Maria's senses like a caress. Dino appeared to be so different to her, but in some ways they were the same.

She broke eye contact and changed the subject, telling him about the village and the playgroup committee and their fundraising activities. As soon as they had finished the meal, she excused herself to tidy up, not wanting to draw out the evening as she would if she'd been dining with a friend. It was difficult to keep her distance from Dino, but she had to be careful. She didn't want him to get the wrong impression of her.

★   ★   ★

After breakfast the following morning, Maria waited until she heard the front door close, then scooted down the hall and peered out of the window at the car park. The black BMW started up and glided away down the lane.

With a sigh of relief, Maria went back to the kitchen and pressed Play on the CD player. She had thought she would never get a moment alone to listen to the *Dirty Dancing* disc. The strains of *Be My Baby* flooded the kitchen and brought a smile to her face. She loved the wonderful romantic plot of the movie, and its soundtrack, but hadn't seen it for ages. As she prepared dough for more rolls she danced on the spot, kneading and humming along with the music. Once she had put the rolls in the airing cupboard to rise, she shook her floury apron out of the door and danced back into the kitchen, practising the salsa steps Dino had taught her.

She laid out the ingredients to make peanut chicken and cut up the chicken breasts, then washed her hands and moved on to the rest of the preparation. As she added each ingredient to the slow cooker, she did a twirl, giggling to herself. She had forgotten what fun dancing could be, how music lifted the spirit.

Once the peanut chicken was in the slow cooker, she retrieved her risen dough from the airing cupboard and put the baking tray in the oven. She swayed her hips and spun around, flapping the tea towel in time to the music . . .

And nearly collapsed with a heart attack at the sight of Dino in the doorway, arms crossed, shoulder rested against the door frame! Heat flooded her cheeks until she knew she must be the colour of beetroot.

'What are you doing back so soon?' she blurted rather rudely. But he didn't appear offended. All he did was hold up a newspaper.

He sauntered into the room, wagging a finger at her. 'Ah, Maria, Maria. You waited for me to go out before you played your music. Do you not want to practise your dance steps with me?' His tone held a note of censure, but she could see he didn't mean it because he was fighting a smile. He dropped his newspaper on the kitchen table and held his hands out to her.

'No, Dino. I'm in the middle of cooking.' She glanced over her shoulder at the counter, searching for a good excuse not to dance with him. 'I haven't finished preparing your dinner.'

He clucked his tongue. 'It is morning, cara. You have all day to do that.'

'My hands are dirty.' She held them out to show him and realised she had recently washed them. Taking advantage of the opportunity, he caught her hands in his and backed up, pulling her into the only clear space in the kitchen, in front of the fridge.

'You remember the steps I taught you?'

'Yes, but . . . ' She had run out of excuses, and he was so persistent it probably wouldn't matter what she said.

He shimmied forwards and back, leading her. Maria looked down at her feet, but she didn't need to. She had practised the steps a number of times that morning and her feet followed his easily. A song ended and another called *Hungry Eyes* started. While the singer carried on about love and desire she looked everywhere but at Dino. Dancing with him to romantic lyrics was very different to practising in silence. Her face was still hot from her earlier blush, and she couldn't see it cooling any time soon.

Although she tried not to look at him, her eyes drifted to his face without permission. He was watching her, a mischievous grin tugging at his mouth, and she couldn't help smiling back. He spun her around and a light, airy feeling invaded her chest as though she could float through the dance.

The notes of a slow ballad filled the kitchen. Dino drew her closer and suddenly there wasn't enough air to catch her breath. Surely he didn't intend to slow dance with her?

He hesitated, and a flicker of uncertainty crossed his face. With a small shrug, he released her hands.

'Now you must practise on your own, and I will read my newspaper.' He grabbed the paper from the table and held it up like a prize as he backed towards the door. 'Tomorrow, we practise again.' Then he pivoted on one foot with the controlled grace of a dancer and headed off along the hall.

Maria leaned back against the counter and put a hand to her racing heart. If he had drawn her into his arms for the slow dance, she wasn't sure what she would have done. But he hadn't. Her relief slowly gave way to disappointment and she silently chided herself for being silly. Slow dancing with the Italian was asking for trouble — even at eleven in the morning.

* * *

Dino took his newspaper through to the small conservatory and sat in one of the wicker chairs so he could see in through the kitchen window. Maria was moving purposefully, doing her chores, her lips forming words he could not hear, singing softly.

The paper lay forgotten on his knees and he released a slow breath. He should stop flirting with her, making her blush, but he enjoyed the game. With her, he could be himself, just as he was with his family and friends back home. He did not have to worry about maintaining an image or giving his fans the wrong impression. It was such a blessed relief to relax and enjoy himself.

In the back of his mind, the pain of knowing he had lost his son still burned, but Maria's gentle care and this quiet, calming place had helped him start to put it behind him.

If only he could stay here — stay with her — but this was a dream, time out of time, not his real life. He bowed his head and pinched the bridge of his nose. Soon he must go back to London, deal with more arguments and conflict with Freddy Short over his future.

But not yet. He did not want to think of that now, to stress over his career. He had a few more weeks before his next tour started, and he would make the most of this time to forget his worries and enjoy himself. With Maria.

* * *

After Maria had prepared Dino home-made vegetable soup for lunch, and served him in the conservatory, she went upstairs for her stint of painting. She had finished the first re-carpeted bedroom and started the second. Nervously, she repositioned the plastic floor covering, watching for eight-legged fiends, but mercifully none jumped out at her.

She was half way through washing down the paintwork with soapy water when Dino appeared in the doorway. Leaning a hand on either side of the door frame, he cocked his hips casually. 'I have done enough walking and thinking now,' he announced suddenly.

'Oh!' Maria's heart pinched at his words. 'Does that mean you're leaving?' Despite knowing it would be best if he left before she got too fond of him, her heart and her head did not agree. Her heart wanted him to stay.

'No, cara. I want to do something useful. I will help you with your painting.'

Maria was so surprised, the wet cloth dropped out of her hand into her bowl, splashing dirty water up her leggings.

'I'm sure you don't really want to paint. Why don't you visit some of the sights? Truro Cathedral is interesting.'

'I want to be with you.' He wandered in and peered at the paint-stained brushes and rollers in the tray on the stepladder.

Maria's pulse raced as she watched him. He couldn't really mean he wanted to be with her! They must be experiencing confusion in the translation.

'You mean you don't want to go out today?' she suggested.

'Yes. I want to relax and talk, enjoy your company. You take my mind off other things, cara.' He held up a brush and swiped the bristles across his palm. 'So I help you paint, and we talk.'

She blinked at him, wondering for the umpteenth time how this could be the same man who had barely spoken two words to her for the first few days of his stay.

'Well, if you're sure, but you can't wear those clothes.'

He held out his arms and looked down at himself. 'You want me to take

74

them off?' he asked with a touch of amusement.

'No! Yes . . . ' She cleared her throat. 'I mean, you need to wear old clothes. Then it doesn't matter if you get paint on them. Dad's things will be too big, but if you don't mind them baggy, his overalls will work.'

Dino shrugged and stepped aside as she moved towards the door. She returned a few moments later with her father's navy coveralls and handed them to him. 'If you slip them on over your clothes, they'll protect you from splashes.'

'I will be a moment.' Dino disappeared and Maria washed a bit more wall before he came back. The old paint-stained overalls were indeed baggy on him, but he still managed to make them look sexy.

She fixed him up with a paint tray and roller and he set to work with the same intense concentration he'd shown when he taught her to dance.

Maria made them both a cup of tea

and brought it up. She had just taken a sip when Dino said conversationally, 'So, Maria, do you have a boyfriend?'

Astonished, she nearly spluttered out her mouthful, and then some of the liquid went down the wrong way and she coughed.

Dino came across the room and patted her back, but she stepped away from his ministrations.

'Look, Dino. I don't mean to be rude, but that's really none of your business.'

'Ah,' he said sagely. 'You do not.'

'I didn't say that.'

'If you had a boyfriend you would tell me. Women like to talk about their men.'

'What gives you that idea?' Maria retorted rather crossly. Because if she were honest, he was right.

'Two sisters and six female cousins.' He paused and angled his head thoughtfully. 'They chatter all the time about their boyfriends.'

'Hmm,' Maria responded, still miffed.

She could give as good as she got. 'Do you have a girlfriend?'

Dino's face fell, and he turned away. Maria gave herself a mental kick. What a stupid thing to ask him when he had turned up here so distressed. He'd probably just broken up with the love of his life or something awful and she'd reminded him.

Dino returned to painting, and for a few minutes neither of them spoke. Then he said softly, 'No. Not for many months.'

So he wasn't suffering from a broken heart — or not one caused by a girlfriend, at any rate. Did that mean he had lost someone else? She cast him a sideways glance as he crouched to paint above the skirting board. It was none of her business why he had come here, or why he'd been upset, but she so badly wanted to know that it was burning a hole in her brain. If she wanted him to open up to her, she had to go first.

'There was someone special a few years ago,' she began, glancing at him.

He didn't look at her, just continued painting. The tension in her shoulders relaxed and she sighed as if she'd been holding her breath forever. 'I went out with him for three years. We talked about getting engaged, but it didn't work out. We wanted different things from life. I guess we grew apart.'

'What did you want that he did not?' Dino said.

Strange. It was the first time anyone had asked her that. Chris and her parents had tried to convince her that she should share Tom's ambition to travel and see the world, to make something of herself, as if staying in Porthale meant that she was wasting her life.

'The truth?' she said, staring out the window at the blue sky. What she really wanted — what she hadn't even admitted to Chris and her parents. 'I want a family. I want my own home to look after, a husband, and children. Lots of children. I want to cook for them, love them, be there for them when they need me, share their joy and their pain.'

She usually kept that ambition to herself because most people didn't even consider it an ambition, but only what happened along the way as you followed your exciting career.

'And your boyfriend, he did not want to be looked after and have children?' Dino asked in an incredulous tone.

Maria put down her paint roller and rubbed her sleeve over her face. She didn't even know what Tom thought of children. They had talked about getting engaged but nothing more.

'I suppose in time he would have, but first he wanted to travel and make a success of his career.'

She'd been so upset with Tom when they split up, feeling he had let her down. Now she realised that his goals hadn't been unreasonable. She and Tom had just wanted different things. They were not on the same page of life. Why had it taken her so long to grasp this?

She glanced across at Dino, who had stopped painting and was leaning on the stepladder watching her. 'So what happened between you and your girlfriend?' she asked.

'She was not who I thought. She did not understand me.'

'Is she something to do with why you ended up here?' Even as the words came out of her mouth, Maria knew she shouldn't be delving into this, but her heart ached when she remembered the lost, desolate expression on Dino's face.

Dino sucked in a breath and rested his head on the ladder. 'I have not shared this with anyone.' He cast her a sideways glance. 'You will never tell, please, even if you are asked.'

Who would she tell? They had no friends in common. She shook her head. 'Of course not.'

'My girlfriend, Rachel, she was pregnant when we parted, but I didn't know.'

Maria's hand flew to her mouth,

dreading the next words out of his mouth. 'She didn't . . . ?'

'No. She had my son and gave him up for adoption.'

The awful tension in Maria's chest loosened for a moment. Then what he'd said hit her. 'Adoption? She gave the baby away without telling you?'

His downcast gaze was her answer.

'But surely that can't be legal without your permission.'

'One would think not, but . . . he is gone, Maria. I never even saw him.'

Tears flooded her eyes, and she found that she had to swallow hard a few times before she was able to speak.

'I'm so sorry, Dino.' She had been imagining all sorts of things but not this. How could his girlfriend have done something so cruel when he obviously wanted his baby?

Dino put down his paint roller and scrubbed a hand across his face. 'I have painted enough. I will walk now, I think.'

Then suddenly he was gone. She

heard his bedroom door, and a few minutes later he strode past the open doorway without acknowledging her.

Why had she dug into his life? He had been happy these last few days and now he was sad again. And no wonder. What sort of a woman did that to a man, especially a caring man like Dino?

4

Maria continued to paint, but her heart wasn't in it any more. Her chest felt tight and achy at the thought of Dino hurting. In spirit she was out on the coast path with him, wishing she could soothe his pain. When he hadn't come home by dusk, she put down her brush, walked through to the front of the house and stared out of the window.

A lone figure sat on the Jacka, facing out to sea. Although twilight made it difficult to determine who it was, something about the figure persuaded her it was Dino. The wind had got up, and he must be cold, sitting there alone — and it was her fault for dredging up the subject that troubled him.

She wrapped the bristles of her paintbrush in a plastic bag so they wouldn't go hard, then fetched the master key and let herself into Dino's room. She paused inside the door, feeling like an intruder, even though she had been cleaning the room for years while guests stayed.

She gathered his leather jacket off the back of a chair and held it to her chest, pressing her cheek against the smooth, warm collar. Then she hurried downstairs, donned her own coat and the trainers she used for walking, and set off down the lane.

Although she could see the Jacka from the Crow's Nest, it took fifteen minutes at a brisk pace to reach it. She had to walk through the village, past the harbour and up the steep coastal path to the rocky outcrop. She kept her fingers crossed that he was still there when she arrived.

Her heart raced as she hurried up the final hill and had to pause for a few moments to catch her breath. At the top she hissed a sigh of relief to find him perched on the highest point, staring out to sea.

'Dino!'

He turned at her voice and smiled. 'What are you doing out here, Maria?'

'I thought you'd be cold. I brought you this.' She handed his jacket across, and he put it on and turned up the collar.

'You are an angel. Thank you, cara.' He shifted over and patted the rock at his side.

She hesitated a moment, then climbed up beside him and wriggled to get comfortable. She hugged her knees against the chilly wind.

'I'm sorry, Dino. I upset you with my questions.'

He shrugged. 'It is not your fault, Maria. I am coming to terms with my loss, but every now and then I am reminded of my son, and I am sad again. The knowledge that he is out there somewhere and will one day call another man papa will always hurt. I just hope that he will be happy and loved as much as I would have loved him.'

Life could be so unfair. Maria

reached out and laid her hand over Dino's. 'It's an old cliché, but they say time heals, and it does. I hardly think of Tom at all these days.'

As she drew back, he caught her hand and lifted it. Her heart jumped at the warmth of his breath, then the brush of his lips across her skin.

'You are kind and sweet, Maria.'

'Not really.' She laughed nervously, trying to ignore the tingles of pleasure racing up her arm.

'You are,' he reiterated, as if that was the end of the matter. 'If you have finished cooking that dinner you started this morning, shall we go back and dine?'

'Of course.' Maria climbed off the rock and waited for him to join her on the path. He jumped down, ran his fingers back through his dark hair and came to her side.

'I'm glad you are here. It is good to have a friend to raise my spirits.' He caught hold of her hand and they walked down the slope. She hadn't been hand in hand with a man since Tom, and it felt strange but nice to have her fingers engulfed in Dino's warm grip.

'I should finish the second bedroom tomorrow,' she said. 'Then I have to shift the furniture back and paint the other two rooms. Could you give me a hand with the lifting?'

'Of course I will. You should not lift heavy furniture. Women have no muscles.'

'I do!' Maria bent her arm to show off her biceps.

Dino squeezed along the top of her arm, which had the effect of making her go all tickly and giggly. 'You have nothing there.'

'Yes, I do!'

'You need muscles like these to move furniture.' He angled his arm and she wrapped her hand around his biceps. She lifted her eyebrows at the firm bulge beneath her fingers, and a delicious image of him shirtless flashed through her mind.

'I was going to ask my brother-in-law to help. Perhaps you and he can move the furniture, and I'll prepare us all a nice dinner. My sister Chris and the girls can come as well and make it a family occasion.'

After the words were out, she realised she'd started to think of Dino as a friend rather than a guest. Maybe more than a friend. And she was helpless to stop the feelings growing.

'A family dinner is good. I would like to meet your sister and her husband.' Dino only relinquished her hand when they arrived at the guesthouse, and he headed upstairs while she went to the kitchen.

Eating dinner with Dino in the dining room had become a habit. As she laid the table, he came in.

'We will have a bottle of wine tonight.' He chose from the wine list and she added wine glasses to the place settings.

Later, when they had finished their meal, they moved to the conservatory and sat side by side in wicker chairs sipping their wine and staring up through the glass ceiling at the stars.

They talked for hours, comparing their childhood experiences, discussing their families and friends, their likes and dislikes, neither of them wanting to end the evening. It was long past midnight when they said goodnight at the bottom of the stairs to her room on the second floor.

Dino kissed her hand and headed along the corridor to his bedroom with a wistful backwards glance.

★ ★ ★

With Dino's help, Maria finished painting the second room the following day, but her brother-in-law Eric had to wait until Friday to get the okay from the chiropractor before he moved the furniture. After lunch on Saturday, Eric's pick-up drew up in the guesthouse car park beside Dino's BMW. Chris, Eric and the girls piled out of the vehicle, laden with the usual bags of baby paraphernalia.

Maria held the front door open and they came inside. Dino leaned against the wall by the dining room, strangely reticent, but when Eric offered a hand, the two men shook and Dino seemed to regain his normal easy manner.

'So, Eric, we lift the furniture and the women they will talk,' Dino said with a mischievous glance at Maria.

'Too right, mate!' Eric slapped Dino on the shoulder, and they headed for the stairs.

'Hang on!' Maria hurried after them. 'I need to tell you where things go.'

'You have already told me, cara,' Dino said, a hint of amusement in his voice.

'I just want to make sure I covered everything.' Maria explained it all again to Eric and watched anxiously as the two men hefted a chest of drawers through to room one.

Chris finally made her way to the top of the stairs with a small girl hanging on each hand. She leaned around the door to admire Dino's rear view and waggled her eyebrows as he bent over. 'Ooh, la la,' she whispered.

'Christine, your husband is right here,' Maria retorted under her breath. 'You're terrible. Come on. The men know what to do now and I have profiteroles in the oven that I need to check.'

Maria took Charlotte's hand while Chris held Poppy's, and they made their way slowly back down the stairs.

Chris sat the girls in front of the television in the sitting room and joined Maria in the kitchen as she removed her dessert from the oven.

'So, how are things going between you and your Italian stallion?' Chris asked.

Indignation flashed through Maria. 'Don't call him that. It's disrespectful.'

'Listen to you with your claws out, protecting your man.'

'He's not my man!'

'Isn't he? I see the way you look at

him. It's obvious you've fallen for him. Are you sure he isn't taking advantage of you?'

'Dino's nice. And he's trustworthy. He wouldn't do anything like that.'

'I don't mean physically taking advantage, Mari.' The amusement had dropped away from Chris's face, and she now looked deadly serious. She placed her hand over her heart. 'I mean he'll hurt you here.'

Maria bit her lip. She had a nasty feeling that Chris was trying to close the stable door after the horse had bolted.

'I can look after myself,' she offered, but even to her own ears she sounded uncertain.

'How does he feel about you?' Chris asked.

Maria shrugged.

'When is he leaving?'

'I don't know.'

'Well, has he said anything about continuing to see you after he goes?' Chris prodded.

Maria shook her head. She'd been in a good mood, but with every question Chris asked, her spirits sank.

'What job does he do?' Chris continued relentlessly.

'I don't know. Can you just leave it, please?'

'Oh, come on, Mari. You must agree I have a point. You two have been cosying up here together for two weeks, and you don't even know what he does for a living.'

'We're not cosying up. And I know lots about him, where he comes from, all about his family and stuff. It's just that his job has never come up, all right?'

But that was a lie. She had asked Dino what he did a couple of times, and he'd avoided answering. She hadn't pursued the matter in case it upset him again.

'I still think he's an actor. I'm sure I've seen him in something,' Chris mused.

'Well, I haven't,' Maria retorted.

'Don't ask him, please.' She didn't want to bring back any memories that might make him unhappy.

Dino and Eric came downstairs a while later, chatting together. Chris helped Maria lay the table and serve the roast beef. Charlotte and Poppy were strapped into high chairs, and they all sat down. The conversation flowed easily, Dino and Eric having a friendly argument about football teams and cars, while Chris and Maria discussed the children and the upcoming play-group fundraiser.

Charlotte dropped her toy monkey and Dino picked it up for her. 'Say thank you, Dino,' Chris said to her daughter.

'Tank 'ou, Dino,' Charlotte copied, then babbled it again and again until they all laughed.

'Trouble with kids is there's no off-switch,' Eric observed.

'It does not get easier,' Dino added with a wry smile. 'The problems just change.'

'You have children?' Chris chipped in, and Maria stilled, her heart faltering. She had tried so hard to avoid subjects that would remind Dino of his lost baby son.

The question seemed to hang in the air unanswered for an eternity, and she imagined how Dino must be feeling, then he smiled and shrugged. 'No children of my own, but many nephews and nieces.'

'Oh, well, that's good,' Chris said.

'Very good,' Eric added. 'Nephews and nieces you can give back at the end of the day.'

They all laughed, but Dino's sounded forced. Chris and Eric chatted and without planning it, Maria's hand crept across the table-cloth to settle over Dino's in silent support. Their gazes met, and gratitude flickered in his brown eyes. She suddenly realised that the talking had ceased and looked up to find Eric and Chris watching them.

Chris was right. Although Dino was a

kind man and would not hurt her on purpose, Maria's heart was already cracking at the thought of losing him.

★   ★   ★

For the next few days, Maria worked hard to finish the decorating and Dino helped. Much of the time they laboured together in companionable silence, and being with him felt so comfortable, so right. Occasionally, the thought that he would soon leave sneaked into her mind, and she shoved it away. She would worry about that when it happened.

At the end of his third week, they decided to spend a day out together to celebrate finishing the painting.

Maria sat beside Dino in the BMW rental car. He switched the radio to a classical music channel as they cruised along the narrow Cornish lanes towards Mevagissey.

'You like this type of music?' she asked, and he nodded.

'It is my favourite. Close your eyes and listen, Maria. It is the sound of beauty and emotion.' He fisted his hand over his heart. 'Do you not feel the music inside you?'

She concentrated and tried to sense what he felt, but the music just sounded too complex to her, the notes all over the place. She preferred a simple repeating melody that she could sing along to.

Maria directed Dino to park on the outskirts of Mevagissey to avoid the narrow main street. They walked arm in arm along the pavement, stopping occasionally to examine the tourist gift and craft items on sale in the shop windows.

The day was grey and overcast with spits of rain, but she didn't care; just being with Dino, holding his hand, laughing and talking, filled her with pleasure.

He wrapped his arm around her shoulders as they walked out to the end of the harbour wall, and cuddled her close when wind rushed in off the sea and buffeted them with fishy-smelling air. Dino examined the fishing boats, commenting on technical things about sailing that meant nothing to her, but he could talk gibberish and she would be happy to listen to the beautiful cadence of his voice. He snapped some photos of her on his mobile phone and she wished she had thought to bring a camera of her own.

Seagulls hung in the wind overhead, calling loudly and periodically skimming low over their heads. 'In the summer the gulls swoop down and steal food from the holidaymakers,' she told him. 'It's quite a problem. Attracting tourists down here is hard enough these days when everything in this country is so expensive — especially when families can hop on a cheap flight and get guaranteed sun in Spain or Portugal.'

'Or Italy,' Dino added.

'Yes!' She punched him playfully on the arm. 'You pinch all the holidaymakers with your warm climate and lovely beaches.'

'If it were up to me, I would send them all back to you.' He laughed. 'But my brother Roberto needs the tourists to visit his restaurant and my papà also. Or he would not sell all his catch.'

'Speaking of fish, how do you fancy trying a fish restaurant here for lunch?'

They stopped outside the mullioned window of a quaint building overlooking the harbour and peered at the menu.

'They do delicious crab topped with melted cheese in here,' Maria informed him.

Seated at a table in the window, they watched the few tourists wander past, and the gulls soar on the wind over the masts of yachts moored in the harbour.

'Mmm, this is so good.' Maria closed her eyes as the delicious mix of melted Cheddar cheese and freshly cooked crab mingled in her mouth. She promised herself that she would try this recipe soon.

When she raised her eyelashes again, she found Dino watching her, his dark gaze intense, and her heart gave a little skip. His hand slid across the red checked tablecloth and he brushed the ends of his fingers over hers, a fleeting contact, but one she felt right down to her toes.

She might have fallen for him unwisely, but little moments like this gave her hope that he returned her feelings. Hope that when he left the Crow's Nest — as he surely would soon — he wouldn't walk out of her life completely.

After lunch, they wandered along the seafront, then cut down a narrow alley towards the main street and browsed the small jumble of shops crammed into every nook and cranny.

Maria halted outside a jewellers and scanned the displays. 'Oh, I love that.' She pointed to a small gold heart on a chain. A simple flower was engraved on the piece with a tiny diamond at its centre, a pinpoint of sparkling light.

'I will buy it for you,' Dino said, stepping towards the door.

'No! I didn't mean for you to do that. It's far too expensive, Dino.' She had commented without thinking, and now she wished she hadn't.

'I can afford it, cara.'

'Please, no. It's okay. I don't want it.' She tugged on his hand, pulling him away from the door. He resisted for a moment, then shrugged and let her lead him along the pavement.

They entered one of the few tourist gift shops that was open out of season, and Maria bought an elastic hair tie decorated with spotted yellow baubles. It would go perfectly with the dress she had found in a charity shop to wear to the hop.

As they ambled along, drips of rain plopped on their heads and quickly became a downpour. Dino pulled her into the doorway of an old-fashioned sweet store that had a Closed sign in the window. Fat raindrops pelted from the sky, hammering the pavement and rattling off the cars that passed. A few people dashed quickly by with their collars up, or fighting the wind to hold umbrellas.

'Great.' Maria groaned. 'This is why all the tourists head to Southern Europe. The inclement British weather.' She shivered. The temperature had fallen and she wished she'd worn her thick sweater as well as a coat.

'I will keep you warm, cara.' Dino wrapped his arms around her and eased her closer to his body. A tendril of heat slid through her, and she looked up to find him watching her. The lyrics to the song *Hungry Eyes* came back to her as the emotion in his brown gaze scorched her. He raised a hand and stroked a finger across her cheek. 'You are so beautiful, Maria.'

It might not be wise; she might be risking her heart, but she longed for him to kiss her.

* * *

Dino trailed his fingers across the silk of Maria's skin, brushing the edge of her lips. He wanted to kiss her more than he had ever wanted to kiss a woman before. He wanted this time with her to last forever, but it was unreal; a fantasy that would slip through his fingers when he returned to his normal life. He had commitments — huge commitments — to the fans who had paid good money for tickets to his upcoming shows, and he would not let them down, however much he wished to remain in this fantasy world he shared with Maria, where he had no worries, no responsibilities, no one making demands on him. He could not simply walk away from his life, from everything he had worked so hard to achieve.

He longed to take Maria with him, but his career meant he must travel from city to city, always on the move, living out of a suitcase, no home or family life. Maria would hate such an existence. It was the antithesis of her dreams. She had broken up with her boyfriend of three years because he wanted to travel.

So, much as Dino longed to kiss her, he would not start something between them that had no future.

But for a little while they could be friends. That would have to be enough.

★　★　★

Now the decorating was finished, Maria and Dino relaxed and enjoyed each other's company. In the mornings, Dino would drive out to get a newspaper, then sit at the kitchen table and read while Maria cooked.

Each time she walked past him, he grabbed her hand and kissed her knuckles, making her laugh. Once she finished preparing food, he switched on the music and they danced around the kitchen like teenagers, living for the moment, no regrets about the past or worries about the future.

After lunch they played Scrabble, which Maria always won as she didn't let Dino use Italian words — or if the weather was nice, they walked along the coast to the next village and shared a cream tea.

In the evening they ate dinner together, then sat in the conservatory and stared up at the stars while they talked, or curled up together on the sofa to watch television.

On the Thursday evening of Dino's fourth week with her, Maria was curled up against him, his arm around her as they watched a romantic comedy. When it finished, she didn't move, enjoying the warmth and security of his presence. Dino flipped through the channels and found a music station playing ballads.

'Dance with me, Maria.' He stood and pulled her to her feet. So far they had only danced to lively tunes, but this was slow, dreamy, romantic. He drew her closer, and gathered her gently against his chest. Maria leaned her cheek on his shoulder and closed her eyes as they moved in a circle, the music flowing over her like a soothing balm. But there was nothing soothing about being in Dino's arms. Her skin tingled and her heart raced at the warm strength of his embrace.

His hand stroked her hair, and he pressed a kiss to her temple. 'After the hop tomorrow night, I'm afraid I must leave.'

Maria's heart lurched painfully and her fingers clutched at his sweater as if she could hang on to him, make him stay. She had known they were living on borrowed time, but had chosen to put it out of her mind.

She had carefully avoided talking about when he would leave or what he did, and he had not volunteered any more details, but she could not let him go without knowing what type of life he was returning to.

She raised her head and met his warm gaze. 'What are you going back to, Dino? What do you do?'

A shadow passed through his eyes, and tiny creases formed between his eyebrows. 'I'm a singer, an operatic tenor.'

'Operatic . . . you mean you sing opera?' She couldn't imagine him doing that. He was too young and vital. Weren't opera singers old and fat? And why was it such a big deal to him that he had avoided telling her until now?

He nodded and gave a tight smile. 'You do not approve?'

'I don't know much about it, that's all. Where do you have to go to sing?'

He threaded his fingers through the hair at her temple, smoothed the strands back behind her ear. 'When I leave here I must go to New York. I am performing *La Bohème* at the Metropolitan Opera House there in two weeks' time and I need to rehearse.'

'America!' Maria bit her lip. She had feared that whatever he did would take him far away, but she hadn't expected it to be that far. 'Will you come back to England after that?'

Dino's gaze slid into the distance and he sighed.

'After New York, I have concert dates in North America before I return to Europe. Then I will spend a week with my family for my mamma's fiftieth birthday. I have not seen them for many months, and I long to go home for a few days. My family has always been very close and they miss me.'

A cold fist of disappointment gripped Maria's heart. She'd hoped he might visit her the next time he had a vacation, but she understood him wanting to be with his family. Maybe he would never come back to Cornwall.

'After that?' she prompted.

'Ah, Maria, Maria. I have a busy schedule. I have to go to Roma, Paris, Madrid, London and many more cities.' He gestured in frustration. 'I do not remember all the places or the order in which I visit them.'

Maria leaned her cheek against his chest, listening to the steady beat of his heart, and blinked away the tears threatening to fall. Dino didn't have time for her in his life. Tom had only wanted to travel before he settled down; this was worse by far for Dino's whole career involved travelling. He would never settle in one place — and certainly not here in the rural depths of Cornwall, with her.

Dino leaned down and whispered in her ear, 'Would you like to visit those cities, Maria?'

'No, I couldn't.' She'd tried travelling and she knew she didn't like it. The Crow's Nest was her home, her future. One day soon her parents would retire, and she planned to take over the guesthouse, hopefully with her husband at her side. But that husband obviously wouldn't be Dino. She had known all along he was not the right sort of man for her — yet in her heart of hearts, she'd still hoped.

After the hop he would leave, and that would be the end of their time together. She might never see him again.

An unbearable pressure filled her chest. She had to distract herself, shake off this awful feeling of loss. He hadn't gone yet. She pulled away from him, grabbed the remote control and swapped the TV onto a dance-music channel. 'Let's practise the salsa for tomorrow night.'

Dino blinked at her, looking bewildered, then seemed to compose himself and smiled. 'Of course, tesoro, of course. We will make sure tomorrow night at the hop is a night to remember.'

5

At six-thirty on Friday evening, Maria carried the trays of finger food she had prepared for the hop out to her car and laid them on the back seat. Dino brought a bag with four cans of lager and a bottle of wine. He held it up questioningly.

'We have to take our own booze as the village hall doesn't have a licence to sell alcohol,' she explained.

He wore smart black trousers, a blue shirt and his leather jacket as he didn't have Sixties clothes. Maria had donned the yellow cotton dress with a full skirt and tight bodice she had picked up for the occasion. Her hair was in a high ponytail secured with the spotty bobble tie she had bought in Mevagissey.

As she locked the front door, Dino pulled a corsage from behind his back and presented it to her.

'Oh, Dino! Thank you.' She put her arms around his neck and hugged him tightly, her heart racing. She had been working towards this fundraiser for months, but now she wished it had never arrived. Tonight was her last night with Dino.

She pulled herself together and stepped back, holding out her arm for him to attach the flowers around her wrist.

'This is lovely, but a bit smart for the village hall.'

'You look beautiful, Maria,' Dino said, his dark gaze gliding over her appreciatively.

She thought beautiful might be too strong a word, and didn't take it seriously. Effusive compliments fell from Dino's lips all the time. She had almost grown used to them, but she was pleased with how she looked tonight. Having her hair tied back suited her, and she had made a special effort with her make-up. She hoped Dino would remember her as being pretty — if he remembered her at all. Travelling as much as he did, he must meet many people, including lots of beautiful women.

In a few months, the chances were he would barely remember their time together. The thought cut through her like a knife; she swivelled away and almost fell into her car seat.

'Maria,' Dino said, resting a gentle hand on her shoulder. 'Are you all right, tesoro?'

'Yes, fine.' She tried to smile and thought she managed convincingly. 'I just tripped.'

Dino sat beside her, his long legs crammed in her little car. It was lucky they only had a few hundred yards to drive to the village hall. Together they unloaded the food and drink, and Dino followed her inside.

Philip was busy organising people to set up tables and chairs around the walls. Maria left the food in the small kitchen and introduced Dino as a friend.

Philip shook his hand and slapped him on the back. 'You've arrived just in time, Dino, mate. Help me set up the tables over there, will you?'

Maria and Philip's wife, Millie, spread tablecloths on the trestle tables as they were erected, and laid out the buffet along one wall while other committee members fetched chairs from the store. Richard, the errant committee member who had been responsible for the music, turned up armed with a Sixties compilation CD after all and checked that the hall's sound system worked.

Maria fished out the *Dirty Dancing* CD from her bag and clasped it to her chest, reluctant to hand it over. This was the music she and Dino had danced to, a little piece of her private time with him that would live on in her memory and her heart forever. She wasn't sure she wanted to share the songs with anyone else.

With a sharp breath of irritation at herself, she passed the disc over.

'Something else to add to the playlist.'

Richard turned it over and scanned the list of tracks. 'Okay, Maria. Looks good. I'll put this on first. There are some lively ones on here to get everyone warmed up.'

Maria watched Dino chatting to people, his hands dancing elegantly through the air as he communicated with his body as much as with his words. The terrible feeling of loss crowded in on her, the darkness waiting to engulf her little pool of happiness. She had only hours left with him . . . mere hours.

Her throat tightened and she swallowed resolutely. There was no point being miserable. She must enjoy this final evening.

Chris bustled in, late as usual, and dumped a plate of sandwiches and four mammoth bags of crisps on a table. 'Sorry I didn't get round to cooking.' She indicated Maria's plates of finger food. 'I knew you'd do us proud, though.'

Chris's friend Tina who had lent Maria the *Dirty Dancing* CD came in behind her with a bottle of wine in each hand. 'Where's this boyfriend of yours I've been hearing so much about, Mari?'

'Over there.' Chris pointed across the room, and Maria's cheeks flamed as the people nearby all turned to look.

'Golly! He's a bit of all right.' Tina eyed Maria with new respect. 'If he turned up on my doorstep, I'd probably let him in as well.'

Maria took Chris's arm and pulled her aside. 'Who have you told about Dino? I'm introducing him as a friend. I'd rather people didn't know he's staying at the Nest.'

'Only Eric and Tina.'

'Well don't tell anyone else, especially not Mum and Dad. I'm going to pretend I had an old college friend to stay because I don't want to charge Dino for his room.'

Chris's eyebrows shot up. 'What about the grocery bill you must have run up?'

'He's more than paid his way by helping me with the decorating,' Maria retorted. She could not imagine asking Dino for money now they were friends.

'Hmm.' Chris looked sceptical. 'I hope he appreciates you, Maria. That's all I can say.'

Maria was saved from having to answer when the speakers crackled and burst into life with the strains of *Be My Baby*, the first track on the *Dirty Dancing* CD. Maria glanced at the clock amazed to find it was eight already, and the doors had opened.

People started coming in, and the place quickly filled. Dino eased through the crowd to her side and clasped her hand.

'Are you ready now to show off your skill on the dance floor, tesoro?' he smiled.

Nobody else was dancing yet and Maria didn't want to be first, especially as it would attract attention to the fact she had Dino with her. 'Let's eat first,' she suggested.

They loaded their paper plates and chatted with Chris and Eric while they ate. Chris pulled a bottle of vodka out of her bag and sloshed a generous amount into Maria's lemonade. 'To oil the wheels,' she said under her breath.

Maria eyed her cup. She rarely drank spirits, but it might give her enough courage to get up on the dance floor and make a fool of herself. After she finished the cupful she felt hot, flushed and a little giggly.

'Will you hide in the corner and waste all our dancing practice?' Dino teased her.

'Course not! I'm ready now.' She dumped her plate on a table and Dino set down his can of lager before helping her to her feet. His warm hands engulfed hers, and his laughing brown gaze caught and held hers as he backed onto the dance floor, drawing her with him. He moved so gracefully compared to the other men, as if he had muscles in places they didn't.

He leaned closer and cupped her

cheek in his palm, pressing his mouth to her ear. 'Now, my beautiful partner, we will show them how it is done.'

She laughed, all tingly from his breath on her skin, and fell into the now-familiar steps of the salsa. As she twirled for the first time Chris and Tina clapped and hooted.

'You are a success, I think,' Dino shouted over the music.

After a few songs, Chris shimmied across to them and tried to copy the dance steps. By now, she had obviously had a few too many spiked lemonades. She grabbed one of Dino's hands away from Maria. 'Teach me, delicious Dino,' she shouted over the music in a bad Italian accent.

Dino cast a questioning glance at Maria and she smiled her assent and released his hand. 'Good luck,' she mouthed. He led Chris and she stumbled through the steps, giggling.

Eric came up behind Maria and put his hands on her shoulders. 'Sorry about this,' he said.

Maria just smiled and danced with Eric for a while beside Chris and Dino, hoping her sister wasn't going to do anything too embarrassing.

A slow song started and Dino passed Chris back to her husband, turned to Maria and drew her into his arms. She flattened her palms on his chest, feeling his muscles move beneath his shirt, and pressed her face into the hollow of his neck. The spicy fragrance of his aftershave reminded her of the first few times she had cleaned his room, before she had got to know him; before she had fallen for him. She would never be able to enter room twelve again without remembering Dino. Her chest tightened, and she squeezed her eyes closed.

'Maria, tesoro,' he whispered in her ear. Then he continued whispering in Italian, his voice low, soft, seductive, and she melted inside. Being with him was equal parts bliss and torture when she knew he was about to leave.

The slow song ended and the tempo

increased again. She eased away from him.

'I need a break, Dino. Let's sit this one out.'

The combination of the alcohol and the other bodies on the dance floor had made her hot. She needed to get outside, get some fresh air. She headed for the door, Dino behind her.

The cool sea breeze hit her like a wake-up slap on the cheeks and her senses sharpened, her ears ringing from the loud music from inside.

'Are you all right, tesoro?'

She fanned her face. 'I'm too hot. Let's stay outside for a few minutes.' She'd had enough of the noise and the people, and just for a while she wanted Dino to herself.

Hand in hand, they wandered across the car park and down the lane to a wooden bench on the edge of the road. She sat and Dino followed suit. From this high up the hill, the view stretched over the cottage roofs. The full moon hung above the sea, painting a golden streak across the rippling water like a living watercolour.

'So beautiful,' Dino said softly.

'Yes, it is.' Maria turned to smile at him, but he wasn't looking at the view. He was staring at her.

His hand lifted to stroke her cheek. 'Maria,' he whispered her name, the sound rolling over her like a caress. 'I will miss you so much, tesoro. I cannot bear to think of it.'

A little burst of hope filled her. 'Come back and see me again, Dino. You must have some free time.'

He dredged up a sigh from the depths of his chest and stared out to sea. 'I do not know when I'll have the chance. My manager keeps my schedule full. I often don't even make it home at Christmas.'

The tiny spark of hope trickled away and left Maria empty and aching inside.

'Perhaps,' he started, then hesitated and looked down at their linked fingers. 'Perhaps you can come with me?'

'You mean to New York?'

Dino pressed a hand to his forehead and closed his eyes as if his thoughts hurt. 'No. New York is not a good place for you to be with me. I will be very busy. I would have to leave you on your own too much.'

Maria found herself shaking her head as she remembered what he'd said about moving from city to city, from hotel to hotel. She couldn't live like that; she didn't want to. She wanted Dino to stay here with her, but when she tried to visualise him running the Crow's Nest with her, she couldn't. He might have helped her decorate and shift furniture, but she had known right from the start that this life was not for him.

'After New York, I will be on tour,' he said, his voice a whisper. 'A few days in each city, then I move on. It is not much of a life, tesoro. Not for me — and not for you, I think.'

They sat silently staring out to sea for what felt like an eternity. Maria's emotions seemed to have hardened

123

into a frigid lump in her chest. She felt empty, hopeless. She shivered in the wind, goosebumps popping up on her skin. Dino put his arm around her and pulled her towards his warmth. She clutched his shirt and buried her face against his chest.

'Maria, amore mio.' His hand smoothed over her hair, soothing, gentling. She could not bear to lose him.

She wondered for a moment if she should just take a chance and go with him. Her parents would be back in a few days to look after the Crow's Nest.

But if she did go to New York, what would she do while he was busy? She'd be left alone in hotels all over the world, knowing nobody, sometimes not even able to speak the language. It would be a million times worse than her trip to Canada.

The thought terrified her.

She had known from the start that Dino was all wrong for her and still fallen in love with him. How foolish! But if she had the chance to do it all again, she wouldn't change a moment of their time together. At least now she knew what it was like to fall in love. She would never forget him.

Maria raised her head. The moonlight limned Dino's features, glinted in his dark eyes, transformed him into a mysterious man of shadow and light. She leaned closer, rested a hand on his shoulder and touched her lips to his.

★   ★   ★

Dino had promised himself he would not kiss Maria, not start something he could not finish, but the sweet bliss of her lips against his was more than any man could resist. He returned her kiss, her body soft and warm in his arms. Leaving her would be the most difficult thing he had ever done. She had helped him overcome the pain of losing his son, yet in coming here, he had exchanged one pain for another far worse; that of losing her.

Maria shivered and he held her closer.

'You're cold, tesoro. We should go home.'

She didn't resist as he helped her to her feet. They walked back to the village hall, his arm around her shoulders to keep her warm. Maria fetched her bag from inside the hall, they climbed into her car and he drove the short distance home.

She clung to his hand as they walked up the path. He took the key from her and opened the front door, not sure what to do next. He wanted to spend every second of the time he had left in Cornwall with her, but he would not take advantage of her affection for him — not when he must leave the next day and might never see her again.

After they entered the hall, she turned into his arms and pressed her face against his neck. 'Don't go, Dino. I want you to stay with me.'

'Maria, amore mio, I wish I could.' Dino held her tight, kissed her hair and for the umpteenth time wished his life could be different. They stood like that for a long time, the only sound the clock ticking in the dining room. She shivered in his arms, her light yellow frock not warm enough for the time of year.

'Come,' he said, leading her towards the stairs.

When they reached the first landing, she held on to him as if scared he would leave her. He had only once been up to the private top floor where she and her parents had their bedrooms, to see the view out of the window, but now he took her elbow and led her up the stairs. At the top, he guided her to her bedroom and opened the door. Her room was much like her; pretty, but not overly fussy.

'Get ready for bed,' he instructed. 'I will make you a hot drink to warm you up.'

She gripped his hand as he turned to leave.

'Come back.'

'Of course, tesoro.'

Dino made two cups of coffee in the kitchen and carried them back to her bedroom. She had changed into pyjamas decorated with pictures of cupcakes and climbed into bed. Wordlessly, Dino handed across her cup and sat on the edge of the bed to sip his coffee. Neither of them spoke. There seemed nothing left to say. He gazed around her room, trying to memorise every detail of what made it unique to her.

When she had finished, she lay down, and Dino stretched out on top of the covers at her side, his arm over her.

'I don't want to go to sleep and waste my last few hours with you,' she murmured.

'Tesoro.' Dino stroked her hair and kissed her forehead.

'Sing to me. The sort of thing you sing in an opera.'

He laughed softly. 'Those songs are much too loud, but I will sing you an Italian lullaby my mamma used to sing me when I was a boy.'

He had not exercised his voice for nearly a month and he started softly, tentatively, very aware that he was rusty. The song brought back memories of his mamma, his happy childhood in Riomaggiore, his brothers and sisters, laughter, a time of hope and excitement before he let himself be drawn along his current career path by Freddy Short's promises of fame and fortune.

Maria closed her eyes, her cheeks flushed from the sudden warmth after being out in the cold.

Dino let his song trail away as the sound of her soft, even breathing filled the room. She had found peace in sleep, but although he lay silently at her side, he could not join her in that sweet oblivion. He pillowed his head on his arm and watched her peaceful expression; imagined what it would be like to stay here with her, and share her idyllic life in Porthale.

But he would not be happy if he were unable to sing, and although he wished it otherwise, she would not be happy if she came with him. It was kinder to make a clean break, let her get over him and find a man who would bring her happiness.

In the early hours, Dino rose from the bed. He could not face a tearful goodbye in the morning. He carefully placed the small gift he had bought her in its tiny red box on the bedside table. He had intended to give it to her before the dance, but somehow the moment had not arrived.

He kissed Maria on the temple, inhaled her floral fragrance and committed it to memory, then rested his hand over hers on the pillow, unable to tear himself away.

But eventually he did. He had to. With a last glance over his shoulder at her sleeping form, he went downstairs and collected the bag he had packed in readiness before the dance.

Maria had refused payment for his room, but he could not leave without at least contributing to the cost of his meals. He left some money on the bureau in the hallway. Then, with a final look around at the place he had called home for nearly a month, the place where he had truly lost his heart, he walked away.

6

Maria's alarm clock rang at seven, and she blinked awake, her mouth dry. *Dino!* The thought shot through her with a jolt as she remembered that it was Saturday, the day he would leave. She raised herself up on her elbows and stared at the bedside table. Two coffee cups stood side by side. He'd been with her when she fell asleep. Where was he now?

She sat slowly, her head aching from the vodka Chris had slipped into her lemonade. Next to the empty cups lay a small red gift box with a square of cream vellum on top.

She picked up the card. On one side was a watercolour of a posy of violets; on the other Dino had signed his name and drawn a heart. She smiled, bittersweet. Inside the box, nestled in cream silk, rested the gold heart pendant she had seen in the jewellery shop in Mevagissey.

A thrill raced through her as she took out the gift and held it up to her neck in the mirror. It was sweet of him to go back and get the pendant, but she wished he'd given it to her in person. She hurried to shower and dress so she could go down to the kitchen and cook him breakfast. This would be the last one, so she wanted to make it special.

She touched the tiny heart, smiling with tears in her eyes. Her emotions swung from pleasure to sorrow and back again, leaving her light-headed. Saying goodbye to him was going to be heartbreaking — but she still had him, if only for a few hours.

When she descended the stairs to the next floor, she noticed the door to number twelve stood ajar. Was he already downstairs waiting for her?

Maria hurried down. Her step faltered at the sight of some twenty-pound notes folded beneath the brass bell on the reception bureau. A terrible sense of foreboding filled her.

The dining room clock ticked loudly in the deep silence. Surely Dino wouldn't have gone without saying goodbye?

She dashed to the front door and pulled it open. The place where his hire car had stood was empty.

'Dino . . . ' The word slipped out on a sob, and her hand rose to clasp the gold heart. Why hadn't he said goodbye? How could he do this to her?

Then she understood. The card with the gift had been his goodbye. But it wasn't enough for her. Not nearly enough. She'd wanted to hug him and kiss him and memorise his face so she never forgot.

Maria backed up and dropped down to sit on the stairs, her hands pressed over her mouth, the hollow ache of loss almost too much to bear. He hadn't even left her his mobile phone number or an email address. She had no way of contacting him. That meant he didn't want to keep in touch with her.

Her gaze drifted into the distance as she remembered their conversation from the previous evening. He had suggested she go with him, and then changed his mind. But she was certain he had feelings for her. So why hadn't he wanted to stay in touch?

* * *

Dino drove for three hours, like a zombie, until he could not keep his eyes open any longer. Then he pulled into a service area, tilted back his seat and fell into an exhausted sleep.

He woke two hours later when someone banged their door against his car. He blinked, eyes gritty with tiredness and misery.

He splashed cold water on his face in the washrooms and bought a double espresso to wake himself up. Then he continued his journey to London.

It was nearly ten-thirty by the time he got going again. Maria would be up and have breakfasted. She'd be baking now

— or maybe she wouldn't, as she no longer had anyone to bake for. His thoughts drifted back to the happy mornings he had spent sitting at her kitchen table watching her cook, inhaling the wonderful fragrance of her creations. She truly was a culinary angel . . . his angel.

When he'd walked out of the Crow's Nest that morning, he had not planned to return. He'd thought it best for both of them, but just a few short hours away from Maria, and he knew he had deluded himself. He was not strong enough to cut her out of his heart. She filled his thoughts, pushing out everything else. If not for his pressing commitments, he would turn round and go back to her.

His priorities shifted as he examined them. If he wanted to see Maria again, he would have to make major changes in his life so he had time to visit her; changes that would take time to implement. Changes that were long overdue.

He dropped off the hire car on the outskirts of London and took a taxi to Freddy Short's office. Freddy's receptionist jumped up as Dino entered, eyes wide. 'Mr Rossellini! Freddy has been trying to reach you for weeks.'

'I know, Trisha.' Dino held up his mobile phone to show he had received every one of the calls and emails. 'Is he busy?'

She picked up the phone and started to speak. A moment later the door to Freddy's office burst open and Dino's manager strode out, tall and imposing.

'Where in hell's name have you been for the last month? You can't just disappear like that! I've had the record company breathing down my neck about the next album. They scheduled a recording studio for you to get started before you go to New York. You've let them down.'

Dino let Freddy's tirade wash over him without reacting. He'd always felt he owed Freddy, owed him for discovering him, developing his career, giving him the opportunity to sing and be successful, but when Freddy had gone behind Dino's back and encouraged Rachel to put his son up for adoption, that debt had been wiped out.

Dino headed into Freddy's office and waited until the older man followed and closed the door.

'I needed a break to consider my future,' he said.

'You won't *have* a future if you pull a disappearing stunt like that again,' Freddy snapped.

Dino gestured dismissively. 'That might have been true once, but not now. I am in demand.'

Freddy swore. 'What's happened to you, Dino? Have you lost your bottle? Can't face the fans any more?'

'Have you forgotten so soon why I walked out?' Dino raised his eyebrows but held his temper.

'Okay, you were ticked off about the kid, but move on. You'll have others.'

Dino wondered how Freddy could

have been his personal manager for five years, worked so closely with him, yet understand him so little. But he wasn't getting into an argument about the way Freddy had handled Rachel's pregnancy. That was in the past, and there was nothing Dino could do to get the boy back. But Maria was his present, possibly his future.

Freddy pushed a sheet of paper across the desk towards Dino. 'Sit down and go through this. It's the record company's suggestions for tracks on the new album.'

Dino leaned over the desk and scanned the paper. He grabbed a pen and went down the list striking out all but two of the song titles. He would no longer agree to record pop songs that anyone could sing in the shower. They were musical fluff, of no substance or merit. A few months ago he would have let Freddy persuade him to sing them, but no longer. He would claim back his artistic integrity, perform only songs that challenged him and gave him pleasure.

'Dino, mate, they're not going to like that. We have some wriggle room on the choice of tracks, but not that much.'

'All right.' Dino tossed down the pen and held up his palms. 'Tell them the next album is cancelled.'

'Whoa! Hang on. You can't do that. I've been negotiating terms on this for six months.'

'I have not signed anything yet,' Dino said.

'I've acted on your behalf.'

'Then you sing the songs, Freddy.' Dino straightened, faced up to Freddy, held his steely hard gaze. 'I will no longer compromise my principles.'

Freddy clenched his jaws and nodded once. 'I'll go back to them and sort this out. You come up with a list of songs, but keep it light. This isn't supposed to be a classical disc.'

'Where is my schedule for the next few months?'

Freddy opened a spreadsheet on his computer and printed it off before handing it to Dino. After *La Bohème* in New York, Dino was booked solid with North American dates in Canada and the States. His breath hissed out in frustration. He had wanted to visit Maria again before he returned to Italy for his mamma's birthday celebration.

After that he was fully committed for months. He scanned the rest of the schedule. Rome, Madrid, Paris, Milan, Barcelona, on and on, city after city. As usual Freddy had him booked tight, with one or two dates at each venue and only a night or two in between. There was no break in which he could visit Maria.

He shook the print-out in the air. 'Are all these dates firm?'

'Most are already sold out.'

Dino pressed his lips together. He wanted to ball up the paper and toss it in the bin. Instead, he folded it and tucked it in his pocket. 'Do not book any more performances. When these are finally done, I intend to return to my roots and join an opera company.'

'That would be a big mistake.' Freddy was round the desk in a couple of strides, a placating expression on his face. 'Who've you been talking to, Dino? Someone's got to you, haven't they?'

'No one has got to me. I have had time to think, and I've made a decision about my future.' Dino headed towards the door. 'I mean it, Freddy. Do not commit me to anything else without my permission.'

* * *

Freddy watched Dino leave, and then picked up the phone and dialled the private investigator he used.

'Gary — you found where Rossellini's been hiding, mate?'

'Had a breakthrough yesterday,' Gary replied. 'He hasn't been partying, 'cause he's only used his credit card once. He spent a couple of hundred quid in a jeweller's in Mevagissey.'

'Cornwall! What in God's name was he doing there?' Then Freddy realised what Gary had said. 'A jeweller's? He must have a bird down there.'

That explained everything. Some woman had got her hooks into Dino and persuaded him to stop touring so she could spend more time with him. Freddy wasn't going to stand for that. He'd put a lot of time and effort into building up Rossellini's career, and he wasn't about to see his investment go down the toilet.

'Get down to Cornwall, Gary, and nose about a bit. I want to know who this bird is and what she's like.'

Women could always be bought off or scared off. Rachel had been difficult, but in the end he'd persuaded her to put the baby up for adoption. This new woman would have her price, and once she was out of the picture, Dino should fall back into line.

* * *

Maria huddled into her thick sweater and zipped up her waterproof coat. She leaned into the driving rain and hurried from the car park into the terminal building at Newquay airport. She hoped her parents' flight was on time. She meant to check on the internet before she started out, but since Dino left, she couldn't concentrate on anything. Her previously good memory had vanished.

In her mind, she continually replayed her time with Dino. Relived every one of his smiles, every touch, every word. Since he'd left, a dull ache of longing burned in her chest.

After her break-up with Tom, she hadn't felt nearly this bad. She hadn't known it was possible to feel this bad. She wished she had told Dino she loved him. She wished she had the courage to go to New York and find him. She wished she could forget him, and go back to how she'd been before he arrived.

The flight from Heathrow was ten minutes late. Maria stared morosely into space while people around her chatted. Then the passengers started coming through the arrival's gate. Maria ruthlessly shoved down the memories of Dino and mentally locked them away. She couldn't mope over him now her mum and dad were home, or they would know something was wrong. The last thing she wanted was an inquisition on why she had let him stay, and what could have gone wrong.

Something *had* gone wrong. He'd stolen her heart!

'Maria, sweetie!' Her mother's voice cut through the ambient drone of conversation. Maria ran forward into her arms.

Her intention of hiding her sorrow collapsed immediately. Tears tightened her throat and filled her nose. She struggled to get out any words. 'Hello, Mum. Did you have fun?'

'Mari, what's the matter? Let me look at you.' As her mother took a half-step back and peered into her face, Maria managed a watery smile. 'I'd like to believe those tears are because

145

you've missed us so much, but somehow I doubt it.'

'I'm fine, Mum,' she mumbled.

'Hello, darling.' Maria's dad came up, pushing a loaded luggage trolley and gave Maria a hug. 'Everything all right at the Crow's Nest?'

'Everything's good. I'm parked out at the front.'

'Come on then,' her dad said. 'I can't wait to get home. I've been dreaming about a nice cup of tea and my own bed.'

Maria's mum put her arm around her shoulders as they headed towards the car. 'Are you sure everything's fine? You don't look fine. You look miserable.'

Maria wiped her eyes on her sleeve and tried to smile. 'Can we leave it for now? I don't want to talk about it. Chris is coming over with the girls when we get home.'

Her mum rolled her eyes heavenwards. 'Dad isn't going to like that. He wants to go to bed.'

'They'll only stay half an hour.'

Maria drove home with her dad nodding asleep in the seat beside her, while her mum sat in the back with a suitcase that wouldn't fit in the boot and started describing the places they had visited on the cruise.

Chris's four-wheel drive was already parked outside when Maria pulled her small car into the Crow's Nest car park.

Her mum jumped out the moment the car stopped and swept first Poppy, then Charlotte into a hug. 'My darling babies, how I've missed you.'

She embraced Chris as well and while they chatted, Maria helped her dad haul the bulging suitcases into the house.

As her mother shepherded the twins in, Chris grabbed Maria's arm and pulled her aside. She was smiling fit to burst, her eyes sparkling. 'I knew I'd seen your Italian before. Look at this.' She pulled a CD case out of her bag and thrust it into Maria's hands.

Maria turned it over. On the front

was a picture of Dino and a beautiful blonde woman. Her heart leaped at the sight of him. Across the front in gold letters it read: *Dino Rossi Sings Show Songs*. Dino had said he was an opera singer, but this was a disc of songs from famous musicals.

She didn't understand. Had Chris somehow made a mock-up CD as a joke? 'What is this?'

Chris released a fraught breath. 'Isn't it obvious? Your Italian is famous. He's a singer.' Chris grabbed the CD from Maria's hands and opened the case. She extracted the small booklet inside and flicked through the pages so Maria could see the pictures of Dino and the blonde woman.

'The blonde bimbo is Rachel Tanner. She won that singing contest a few years ago. You must remember her, surely.'

Rachel! A shock ran through Maria. Was this the woman who had given birth to Dino's son and put him up for adoption?

Maria swallowed hard as she examined the photographs of Rachel Tanner. In a glittery sheath dress with cascading waves of honey-blonde hair, she was glamorous and beautiful. If this was sort of woman Dino dated, Maria had no hope that he would even remember her!

'Well?' Chris prompted, her voice tight with excitement. 'Didn't I tell you I recognised him? I could hardly believe it when Tina brought this over.'

'Thank you,' Maria said, not knowing what else to say.

'Did he tell you he was a singer?'

'Sort of.' Dino hadn't exactly lied to her, but he had definitely been economical with the truth, and she didn't want to discuss it with Chris. 'Can I borrow the CD?'

'Of course. I'm sure Tina won't mind. I listened to it before I came over. He's really good, you know.'

Maria tried to smile but Chris looked disappointed. Obviously she'd expected a more enthusiastic response. Maria tucked the CD into her handbag and followed Chris inside.

She struggled to focus on her mum's stories about their cruise. Her mind kept slipping away into a dark pool of confusion over Dino. They all had cups of tea and sampled the blueberry muffins she had baked earlier. Then her dad yawned and headed upstairs. A few minutes later, her mum saw Chris and the girls off and came back to the kitchen where Maria was listlessly washing up cups.

'I'm worried about you, Mari. Last time I saw you like this was when you came back from Canada. You know you can talk to me if there's something wrong, don't you?'

'I know, Mum.'

'By the way, where did that bunch of twenties in the bureau come from?'

Heat flared in Maria's cheeks. She had intended to bank the money Dino left but had forgotten. 'I had a friend to stay for a few days. He gave me a contribution towards the food.'

Her mother's eyebrows rose. 'He must have eaten a lot. There's nearly four hundred pounds there. Who was this friend? It wasn't Tom, was it?'

'Tom? Gosh, no! Tom's history, Mum, ancient history.'

'It's just that the last time I saw you moping around like this was over him.'

'Look, I'm fine. Can we just leave it?' Maria grabbed a tea towel and a wet mug and gave it her full attention.

For long moments her mother scrutinised her, then she sighed and pressed a kiss on Maria's cheek.

'I'm off to bed. I've no idea what time my body thinks it is right now, but I need sleep. I doubt you'll see me or Dad until tomorrow morning. Good night, love.'

'Night, Mum. It's great to have you back. Sleep tight.'

Maria kept drying mugs until she heard her mother's footsteps on the stairs, then collapsed into a chair at the kitchen table. The exact chair Dino had sat in so many times while she cooked and they chatted. She pulled the CD out of her handbag, and stared at it.

'Dino Rossi.' She whispered the name to herself. Rossellini was a bit of a mouthful. He must use Rossi as a stage name.

She didn't know what to think, what to feel. Why had he told her he was an opera singer when he was obviously far more than that? How many music CDs did he have out? She went to the small office off the hallway and booted up the computer. As she waited for it to open, she rubbed her gritty eyes. She hadn't slept well since Dino left. She almost wished she hadn't answered the door the day he turned up. If she had started the painting upstairs, she might never have met him.

Once the computer opened, she went to a website and typed in Dino's name. Three CDs came up; the *Show Songs* one, another called *The Voice of Romance* and one titled *Just Like Heaven*. She ordered all three and paid extra for next-day delivery.

Then on a whim, she typed his name into a search engine. It came up with over three million hits, including photos and videos. Maria rocked back in her chair, her heart thumping as she scanned the list. She clicked on a video link and, barely breathing, watched a clip of him singing an operatic song. He had a beautiful voice, an incredibly powerful voice, considering how softly spoken he was.

She searched for images. Page after page of photos of Dino appeared; Dino singing, Dino at celebrity events with a variety of glamorous women on his arm — especially the beautiful, blonde Rachel — Dino accepting awards. Maria felt as though she had fallen into an alternative reality. This was not her Dino; not the man who had danced her round the kitchen and taught her to salsa. He was famous, almost certainly loaded. He must be used to exclusive hotels, the best of the best. And he had stayed here, eaten the food she cooked. He'd worn her dad's overalls and helped her paint the bedrooms!

Unable to reconcile the two disparate versions of Dino, she stared at a photo of him on a red carpet with the ever-present Rachel at his side. Maria had thought he had feelings for her, but why would a man like this be interested in her?

No wonder he had slipped away without leaving his phone number or email address. She clasped the tiny gold heart at her throat. Dino hadn't been himself when he came here, or he would never have chosen to stay at the Crow's Nest.

She had helped him during a difficult time and he'd been grateful. What she had taken to be affection on his part was probably just gratitude.

The more she thought about his behaviour, the more she admitted he hadn't acted like a man in love so much as a man who wanted to forget his woes and relax for a few weeks. He'd had many opportunities to kiss her and never had. She had been the one to kiss him!

She rested her head in her hands and closed her eyes. She had made a fool of herself. Worse still, she had let her emotions carry her away and lost her heart to a man who was so out of her league that it was embarrassing.

7

Maria shut down the computer and paced up and down the hall. She had to get out and walk off some of the stress and tension or she would implode. She understood now why Dino had walked so much the first few days he'd stayed here.

She pulled on a thick sweater, gloves and a woolly hat, then donned her waterproof coat and some boots. The weather had suddenly grown cold after Dino left, almost as if it was mirroring her mood. After locking up, she strode down the lane heading for the coast path. Her mind roiled with thoughts, doubts, memories. She wished she could switch her brain off and have a break from this mental turmoil.

Half way down the guesthouse drive, she met a man in a long black overcoat with a camera and binoculars hanging round his neck. She was so absorbed in her thoughts, she nearly bumped into him. He peered at her curiously, and she stepped back as a shiver ran down her spine. He had a ruddy face, greying hair and puffy bags under his eyes as though he hadn't slept in a long time.

'The guesthouse is closed,' she blurted, not quite sure what it was about him that spooked her.

He rubbed his hands together and nodded. 'I don't want to stay. I was just walking up the hill for the view.' He tapped his binoculars. I'm a bird-watcher.'

He had a pronounced London accent. Birdwatchers occasionally stayed at the guesthouse, but Maria had never seen one dressed like this man. He looked as though he belonged on a city street.

'This is a private lane,' she said, hoping that he would take the hint and go away.

Instead he grinned. 'You own the guesthouse, then, love?'

She really didn't want to talk to him

or give him any information, but ingrained courtesy made her answer. 'It belongs to my parents. Now if you don't mind, I'd like to continue my walk.'

'Don't let me keep you.' He waved her past as though he was directing traffic. She continued on, glancing over her shoulder at him. 'All right if I take a look at the view from up there, love, is it?'

Without waiting for her answer he continued up the hill towards the Crow's Nest. Maria halted and stared at the man's back, unease trickling through her. Instinct told her he was bad news, but just how, she didn't know. She had locked up, so he couldn't get into the guesthouse. Short of following him and telling him to go away, she couldn't do much.

With a frustrated huff, she resumed her march down the hill.

At the entrance to the lane a car was parked, half blocking the narrow road into the village. Even though she depended on tourists for her livelihood, they still annoyed her sometimes with their lack of thought for the locals.

She paced along the main street, keeping her gaze down, not wanting to catch anyone's eye and feel obliged to stop and chat. She continued through the car park at the top of the harbour and up the coast path to the Jacka. When she arrived, she sat on the rock she had shared with Dino many times, closed her eyes and tried to imagine he was sitting beside her.

The memories of Dino were so clear and sharp they cut. She would need to do a lot of walking before she worked him out of her system, if that was even possible. In four short weeks, he had penetrated to the very core of her being. She glanced back towards the Crow's Nest, and her breath jabbed with shock at the sight of a figure walking round the corner of the building. The Londoner was in the guesthouse garden!

Her parents were asleep upstairs.

159

Had the man tried to break in? Her heart hammered in her ears as she narrowed her eyes to see if he was carrying anything. The figure stopped, turned her way, and raised his hands to his face. It looked as though he was holding his binoculars or camera and staring right at her.

* * *

Freddy Short opened the email from his PI Gary and scanned the message. The man had tracked down the place Dino stayed in Cornwall to a fishing village called Porthale and spoken to a bird who could be the love interest. Freddy clicked on the link to open the private page where Gary posted digital photos, and typed in his password.

He scrolled through the images one by one. The tiny village looked like the back of beyond. Freddy couldn't imagine why anyone in their right mind would visit the dead-end place. There were no shops, hardly any people. It was just a lot of grass and barren rocks.

Then he came to the first image of a young woman walking down the village street. She was too far away to make her out. There were a few more pictures of her, but her face was grainy, the photos obviously taken from a distance. She didn't look much to write home about. She was wearing an anorak, for goodness' sake! He half wondered if Gary had made a mistake, but the man was normally good at his job.

'Dino, Dino,' Freddy whispered to himself. 'What were you thinking, mate?'

Freddy enjoyed discovering talented young singers to mould into successful professionals, and Dino Rossellini was his greatest prize. Whatever the indefinable thing that bestowed star quality, Dino had it in spades. The Italian could do so much better than this ordinary girl from nowhere.

Freddy would not allow Little Miss Nobody to disrupt Dino's career and cut short the very healthy revenue stream that flowed in from the Italian. If she really did have her claws into Dino, then Freddy would buy her off.

But he wasn't about to pay out unless he had to. Given a little encouragement, Dino would probably forget her anyway.

What Freddy needed was someone out in New York to keep Dino occupied — and he knew just the girl.

Freddy dialled Rachel's mobile number and drummed his fingers on the desk. 'Rachel, love,' he said when she answered. 'I've got a little job for you. I've arranged for you to join Dino in New York. He'll need a partner for the social functions he has to attend, and you can do a couple of cable television spots while you're there to raise your profile in North America.'

'Did he ask for me?' she said, tentatively.

'Yes, darling. He can't wait to see you.'

Freddy winced at the lie. He had a soft spot for Rachel, and he knew the pregnancy and adoption argument with Dino had knocked her sideways. She was still in love with the Italian, and it would suit Freddy if they got back together. Having them as a couple made for great publicity.

Dino and Rachel were both beautiful people. They had chemistry, which was why they performed so well together. Freddy planned to sit back and let nature take its course.

* * *

Dino was talking to the musical director of *La Bohème* when one of the Metropolitan Opera House stage hands came up to him and interrupted. 'Excuse me, there's a woman waiting for you in your dressing room, Mr Rossellini.'

Maria! He had left instructions that if a British woman asked for him she should be shown to his dressing room, but it had been an unlikely dream that Maria would come after him. He made his excuses and hurried along the corridor to the dressing rooms, a stupid smile fixed on his face.

He burst through the door, heart racing with anticipation and his step faltered. Rachel sat in the seat before his mirror examining her nails.

It took him a moment or two to mask his disappointment.

He forced a smile and went forwards to kiss her on both cheeks. It was crazy, really; Rachel was without doubt the most beautiful woman he had ever met, and he knew she had feelings for him, but he couldn't reciprocate. He'd tried. They worked together often, and he had got to know her well before they started a relationship a couple of years ago, but something was missing. He did not love her and knew he never would.

Breaking off the relationship had been difficult. When Freddy sent Dino on a solo tour and had Rachel occupied elsewhere, Dino had been grateful. Now he knew Freddy hadn't been trying to be thoughtful, but making sure Rachel's pregnancy was kept secret. Freddy always had an angle.

'Are you happy to see me, darling?' Rachel asked tentatively, fiddling with a length of golden hair.

Dino put extra effort into his smile and hugged her. 'Of course, cara.' She might appear self-assured, but he knew her well enough to see behind the mask. She was anything but confident. She doubted herself continually; her looks, her voice, her popularity. She needed reassurance, and Dino was used to offering it. Freddy had arranged for Dino to be her mentor in the final rounds of the talent contest that shot her to stardom. Dino had nurtured her through that experience, bolstering her confidence at every turn. He had come to believe that was partly why she thought she loved him.

'What brings you to New York, Rachel?'

She sat on the edge of his dressing table unit and wrapped her arms around her slender body. She looked as though a strong wind would blow her away. 'Freddy has arranged for me to do a couple of cable shows.'

'Which ones?'

Rachel shrugged and twisted her rings on her fingers.

'You should call him, cara, find out the details. You don't want to miss the dates.'

She pulled her phone out of her bag. 'Will you come with me, Dino? I never know what to say in interviews.'

Dino released a breath. He would get sucked back into Rachel's life if he wasn't careful.

'If I can. Remember I'm rehearsing for *La Bohème* and we're on a tight schedule. The first performance is in two weeks.'

'We're still touring together when you finish?'

'That's what Freddy says.'

She looked down and worried her lip with her teeth. 'Have you forgiven me about the baby, Dino? I didn't mean to make you angry. I only did what Freddy said you'd want.'

She looked so forlorn and miserable that Dino stepped forwards and pulled her into his arms. She clung to him like a child, and Dino cursed Freddy anew for interfering in their lives. He wanted to tell her that she should have spoken to him and not believed Freddy's advice, but that would upset her more and achieve nothing. Although he still hurt at the thought of his lost son, it was time to let go of his anger over the adoption.

He kissed Rachel's hair, the smell of her perfume so familiar. 'It's all right, cara. I know you tried to do the right thing, and I'm sure our son is happy with his adoptive parents.'

As if he'd said the magic words, Rachel's face lit up. She gave him a quick kiss on the lips, taking him by surprise, then tottered back on her heels, grabbing her bag from the dressing table. 'I'll call Freddy tomorrow. Let's go and celebrate.'

Dino frowned, wary of her sudden

change of mood. 'Celebrate what, cara?'

'Being friends again, of course.'

As long as that is all she expects of me, Dino thought, as he slipped on his jacket.

Rachel clung to his arm as they walked, told him about her flight and the show she'd been working on in London. They stepped through the stage door to be met by a small crowd of photographers. Flash lights went off in their faces and only long training kept Dino smiling. In front of the cameras, Rachel bloomed like a rose in the sun. Flicking back her hair and pulling up the collar of her faux fur coat, she smiled coyly.

'How are the rehearsals for *La Bohème* going, Mr Rossi?' someone shouted.

'Very well. I'm looking forward to opening night.'

'Are you performing in the opera as well, Ms Tanner?' a woman asked Rachel.

Rachel clung to Dino's arm and

giggled. 'I'm just here to keep Dino company.'

The photographers all laughed, and one of them joked, 'Then he's a lucky guy!'

'Well, I'm hungry, so if you don't mind, we'll be on our way,' Dino said tightly. Wanting to get away before Rachel said anything else that might come back to haunt him later.

The crowd parted and, with a burst of camera flashes, Dino ushered Rachel to the waiting limo. They returned to the hotel where they were both staying and agreed to meet in the lobby in an hour.

Dino showered and changed, and as always happened when he had quiet moments alone, his thoughts turned to Maria. He tried to imagine her here with him and found he couldn't. She would be like a fish out of water in the big city. She'd hate the photographers, the lack of privacy. However much he missed her, it was best that she had not come. Far better that he visit her away from the eyes of the press — in her world rather than in his.

He picked up his phone and scrolled through the photos he had taken of Maria in Mevagissey. The ache of missing her was as tight as a fist squeezing his heart. He had programmed the Crow's Nest telephone number into his phone and numerous times since he left Cornwall, he'd thought of calling her, but what would he say? That he missed her and wanted to be with her? He would only upset her because it was not possible for them to be together.

But what if he took too long to return and she forgot about him or found another man — one who would put her before his career, as she deserved?

'Argh!' He tossed his phone on his bed and pinched the bridge of his nose. Why was life so complicated? It would be much easier if he fell in love with Rachel, a woman who shared his lifestyle and understood what it involved. Perhaps he should just forget Maria and give Rachel a second chance? But even as the thought entered his mind, his heart dismissed it.

Dressed for dinner, he went down ten minutes before he was due to meet Rachel and perused the boutiques in the hotel until he found one selling postcards. He selected a card and bought a stamp. Then he withdrew from his wallet the credit-card sized picture of the Crow's Nest that had contact details on the back. He copied the address onto the postcard and simply wrote, 'Missing you' and signed his name.

'What are you doing, Dino?'

He had been so absorbed that Rachel's voice behind his shoulder made him jump. 'Nothing,' he replied automatically, which was daft as he was obviously writing a card.

'Who's that for?' Rachel reached around him and tried to pick it up, but he pushed it in his pocket while he tucked the guesthouse business card back in his wallet.

'Come,' he said, trying to distract her. 'Where would you like to go for dinner?'

She mentioned a very expensive restaurant that would almost certainly be booked solid, but Dino wasn't about to disappoint her. He'd find a way to secure a table. As they left the hotel, he slipped the postcard and a tip to the doorman.

'Mail this for me, please.'

Then he escorted Rachel to a cab and prayed he could walk the fine line of keeping her happy while maintaining his distance.

* * *

A few days later, Maria went down for breakfast to find her mother bustling around the kitchen. Maria stood in the doorway with a vague sense of discomfort. She had got used to the kitchen being her domain while her parents were away. Now she was back to the role of daughter sharing her mother's space.

'Morning, darling. Do you want toast or cereal?'

Maria noticed a cardboard package open on the table and two CDs beside it. She grabbed it and checked the address.

'Mum, you've opened my package. Don't I get any privacy in this house?'

'Don't be over-dramatic, Mari. It's only a couple of music discs, that's all.'

'That's not really the point, is it? You opened my mail.'

Her mother rolled her eyes heavenwards. 'Tea or coffee?'

'Coffee, please.' Maria sat and read the invoice from the package. 'What happened to the third CD?'

'Oh, I listened to it before you came down. It's still in the player. Do you want me to turn it on?'

'Not now.' She didn't want to share Dino with her mother!

'That young Italian certainly has a lovely voice,' her mother continued. 'I wouldn't have thought his music was quite your sort of thing, though. What made you order it?'

Maria's cheeks warmed and she silently berated herself for being stupid. 'Chris's friend Tina lent me the show songs disc. I liked it, so I bought the others as well.'

'Strange coincidence. I read an interview with Dino Rossi and his girlfriend Rachel Tanner in the in-flight magazine on the way home from Florida. They sound like a lovely couple. They met when he was her mentor on that talent show she won a few years ago.'

Maria did not want a lesson on Dino's life from her mother. 'Where's Dad?' she asked, changing the subject.

'Gone to Truro to bank the cash that friend of yours left, and run errands.'

Maria ate some cereal and read the track lists on the CD covers, then checked out the booklets inside with the song lyrics and pictures of Dino.

The photos made her yearn to see him again. As soon as she had finished breakfast, she took advantage of her dad's absence and nipped into the office before he returned, closing the door behind her. She booted up the computer and searched Dino Rossi, pulling up the now familiar list of links. She couldn't go a day without looking at photos of him. She was like an addict needing her Dino fix. She found her favourite video of him performing and stared rapt at the screen while he sang.

Everything about him was so familiar; the elegant way he moved his hands, his facial expressions, the tiny gestures he made that tugged at her heart. This was torture, seeing him but not being with him. She leaned forwards, her chin on her hand, and lost herself in her memories of him.

Suddenly the door opened behind her, and she nearly jumped out of her skin. She scrabbled for the mouse and closed down the video, then cast a furious glance over her shoulder at her dad as he riffled through a filing cabinet.

'All right, love?' he said, finding what

he wanted and shutting the drawer.

'Yes, Dad.'

He wandered over and kissed the top of her head, then disappeared out the door, leaving it open.

She was lucky it was her dad who had walked in and not her eagle-eyed mother, who would have noticed what she was watching. Maria flopped back in her chair and stared at the calendar on the wall. Her parents had been home for five days, yet it felt like forever.

Before they went away, she hadn't noticed that they treated her like a child. But after the month here alone with Dino, she realised she wanted her own space, her privacy.

'Maria, darling,' her mother said, poking her head in the door, 'when you've finished, could you come into the kitchen for a few minutes? Dad and I want to talk to you about the future.'

A jolt of excitement shot through Maria. A few months ago, her parents had started discussing retirement. Maria would be sad to see them leave the Crow's Nest, but she was ready to take over the place. She already had a few changes and improvements in mind — and if she was in control, she could invite Dino to stay if he ever contacted her again.

She bounded out of her chair and headed into the kitchen. Her mother refilled the coffee cup Maria had used at breakfast and then sat down facing her.

'Dad and I had lots of time to think on the cruise. We've worked hard over the years, especially in the early days when the Crow's Nest was open in the winter. When you were little, we only closed for two days at Christmas each year. We couldn't afford to close with a mortgage to pay. But all that is behind us, and it's time to wind down.'

Maria held herself still and tried to control her bubbling excitement. 'So you're retiring?'

'I think so, love.' Her dad smiled, but he looked sad. 'We'll be sorry to leave the place, but Mum is keen to travel, and we want to do it before we get too old to enjoy ourselves.'

'I think it's a wonderful idea.' Maria gripped his hand and squeezed. She knew her dad was a homebird at heart, like her, and leaving the Crow's Nest would be more of a wrench for him than for her mum. 'I'll take care of the place for you. You know how I love it.'

Her mum and dad exchanged a worried look, and foreboding shivered through Maria.

'I know we talked about taking out a loan on the place to realise some of its value, but we've taken financial advice, and I don't think it's going to work.'

Everything inside Maria froze. 'What do you mean?'

'We're going to sell up, love. The Crow's Nest is our pension, you see.'

Maria's hand went to her heart and for long moments she couldn't speak. Her chest burned as though all the air had been sucked out of her lungs.

'I don't want to leave,' she whispered.

'This is my home too. You can't just sell it. Please.'

'I'm sorry, love.' Her dad patted her arm. 'The truth is, we need the money. Mum wants to go on a world cruise, and it doesn't come cheap. And if we're going to buy another home we must sell this one.'

'What do you expect me to do?' Maria's voice rose on a note of panic. The guesthouse was her life, her future. She didn't have anywhere else to go.

'It'll be good for you to move on,' her mum said. 'You need to get out and see the world, meet a young man, make something of your life.'

'But I planned to run the Crow's Nest with my husband — raise my kids here, like you did.'

'What husband?' her mother asked softly.

Maria bit her lip.

'You've been down here burying your head in the sand since you broke up with Tom. There's a world out there, darling. That's where you'll meet a husband. Not here.'

'I've been out in the world,' Maria said defensively. 'I spent three years at Uni. And I went to Canada with Tom.'

'Three months in Canada is not seeing the world, Maria,' her mother replied.

Tears blurred Maria's vision, and she blinked them away. 'But this is where I want to spend my life.'

Maria's mother reached out and gently stroked the hair back behind her ear. 'If we let you hide down here, we won't be doing you any favours, Mari. This is for your own good, really.'

Maria held tight to her wildly fluctuating emotions. Shouting and screaming would not convince her parents she was a responsible adult capable of running the guesthouse.

'Look,' she said in a controlled voice, 'give me a year operating the place alone. I'll show you I can make a go of it. I'll bring in enough profit to fund your trips.'

'But not enough for us to buy

another house.' Her mother gave her a sad smile. 'It's all decided, darling. We have two commercial estate agents coming round this afternoon to give us a valuation.'

She reached across the table and pulled a stack of estate agents' house details out from under a newspaper. 'And when your dad went into town this morning, he signed us up with some agents to start looking for a new home.'

Maria's last shred of hope unravelled. They had made their decision and nothing she said would change their minds.

She'd lived her whole life at the Crow's Nest. Porthale was her home. She had no idea where to go . . . unless she followed Dino. But she didn't even have the money to fly to New York. Her parents had never paid her a wage; they simply paid her living expenses. All this time, they had treated her like a child — and she hadn't realised until now.

Her dad picked up a catering

magazine and placed it on the table before her. 'There are five pages of jobs in the back. Why don't you take a look? I'm sure a young woman with your qualifications and experience will find a job in no time.'

'We'll give you money for a deposit on a flat,' her mum chipped in. 'You'll enjoy being independent.'

Maria stood, her chair scraping on the floor tiles with a grating screech, and headed to the office. She shut the door behind her and leaned back against it, her hand over her eyes. What was happening to her life? First Dino had arrived and tied her emotions in knots; now this.

She plonked down in the office chair and half-heartedly searched for flights to New York. There were none from the local airports, which meant travelling up to London. After doing a rough cost calculation, she tossed down her pencil in disgust. The only way she could go to New York was if her parents paid the costs. And by now, Dino had probably forgotten all about her.

The next few days passed in a stunned haze as Maria came to terms with her uncertain future. Many times she considered asking her parents for money to buy a ticket to New York, but each time she worked up the courage to face the inevitable grilling on why she wanted to go, her own doubts cut in.

Dino would have left his phone number if he wanted to see her again. He hadn't even said goodbye!

But then she touched the tiny gold heart around her neck, remembered the way he had stroked her hair, the way he had watched her as she cooked, and she didn't know what to think. He definitely had feelings for her, but what sort of feelings?

8

Her parents had been home for a week when Maria went down to breakfast to find her mother looking at a postcard.

'Who do you know in New York, darling?'

Her mother turned the card over to read the message, and Maria darted forwards and snatched it from her hand. A quick glance at the front confirmed it was a picture of the Lincoln Centre in New York where the Metropolitan Opera House was situated. With a thundering heart, Maria turned the card over to read the back.

Dino hadn't written much, but what he had put was enough. He missed her!

She collapsed into the chair with a hand over her mouth and tears of joy in her eyes, momentarily forgetting her mother's curious appraisal.

'Is that from a boy?'

'A man, Mum. He's a man.'

'So who is this mystery man?'

'Someone who's important to me. Look, can I have some money?' Maria finally tore her eyes away from Dino's handwriting to meet her mother's worried gaze. 'I want to go to New York to see him. I'll need to pay for travel up to London, the flight, a hotel and probably some other stuff I haven't thought of yet.'

'Well, I don't know . . . ' Maria's mother frowned at her. 'Isn't this a bit sudden, darling? When did you meet him?'

'I don't ask for much, Mum! I've worked for nothing more than board and lodging for years. That must give me some credit to call on.'

'We paid you a bit more than board and lodging,' her mother said indignantly. 'What about your car and your clothes?'

'Yes, I know. I'm not saying you didn't look after me, but I've never had a wage to allow me to save for a holiday. A few days ago you told me I need to

185

see more of the world. Well — I want to see New York.' *As soon as possible,* she added silently.

'Let me have a chat with your father. We're talking about a few thousand pounds, I expect. That's not small change.'

It was considerably less than her parents had spent on their recent four-week cruise in the Caribbean, but Maria didn't voice that opinion.

She went to the office and started searching for flights that left in the next few days, hoping for a late deal. If Dino was missing her, that meant he wanted to see her! The thought of making the trip to America was daunting, but if she could see Dino again, she would step outside her comfort zone.

★   ★   ★

A few days later, Maria pulled her suitcase out the doors of New York's JFK international airport with her sister at her side. Maria's mum and dad had been reluctant to fund her trip, but Chris had found a four-night deal and loaned Maria the money on condition she could come along. Maria was too focused on Dino to think about the shopping blitz Chris planned, but she was grateful to her sister for the loan and the moral support.

Maria felt light-headed with tiredness after travelling for so many hours, but the thought of seeing Dino fizzed through her like a large dose of caffeine.

They climbed into a yellow taxi and told the driver to head for the Metropolitan Opera House. Maria was lulled into a daze as the vehicle slid through traffic while blues music played softly on the radio. They had been going for nearly an hour when Chris squealed with excitement. 'I can see the Empire State Building!'

Maria peered out and excitement ticked in her chest, her body a mass of jangling nerves. Soon she would see Dino again. Or she hoped she would. She hadn't let herself dwell on the problem of making contact with him.

Finally the taxi halted at the bottom of some wide, shallow steps that ran the length of the plaza outside the Lincoln Centre.

'We're here, ladies.' The taxi driver pointed across the open space to a spectacular building with five massive arches along the façade.

Maria paid him and he fetched the bags from the boot.

'Wow, this place looks like a modern day palace. It's fantastic,' Chris breathed.

Maria placed a hand over her bounding heart and stared at the building. Chris was right; it was magnificent. They pulled their cases up the steps and gazed at the imposing buildings that lined three sides of the Lincoln Centre plaza.

'Dino's here,' Maria said a little breathlessly. 'I just know he is.' Excitement energised her as she set off at a brisk pace, tugging her case behind her.

'Hang on!' Chris traipsed after her,

wobbling on the heels she'd worn. 'My feet are killing me.'

'I told you to wear flat shoes for travelling,' Maria said, scuffing the toe of her comfortable trainer against the ground as she waited for her sister to catch up. At a more restrained pace, they walked across the plaza side by side.

At the entrance to the opera house, she asked a security guard for directions to the stage door. As instructed, they headed down a staircase and an escalator to the underground parking level and found the corridor he'd directed them to.

'This is a bit naff,' Chris said wrinkling her nose. 'I thought the stage door would be really flash. Surely they don't make the stars come in through the parking garage. It's more like a tradesman's entrance.'

Their footsteps echoed along the concrete floor, then Maria halted at a set of double doors that led into the bowels of the opera house. Her stomach churned like a washing machine on spin cycle.

'How are we going to get in?' Chris asked.

'Knock, I guess.' Maria raised her hand and gave four hard thumps on the door. 'That should get someone's attention.'

Chewing her lip, Maria waited for the door to open. It didn't.

'Blast,' she whispered.

'Maybe we should ask at the box office,' Chris offered.

Maria had hoped that if she could make her way to New York then everything would fall into place, but even if Dino was inside the opera house, she might not gain access. What she'd really done was come racing over here on a wing and a prayer with no idea how to contact him. A sigh hissed out between her lips and Chris's hand settled on her arm.

'Don't worry. We've got four days to contact him.'

Suddenly four days didn't sound very long.

They turned to head back to the lobby but had only gone a few yards when the stage door opened. Two men in overalls came out chatting. Maria left her case and dashed back. 'Excuse me. I need to see Dino Rossellini. Is it all right to go in?'

One of the men held the door open for her. 'Go for it.'

'Where are the dressing rooms?'

He shrugged.

'Wow, that was lucky!' Maria caught the door and held it open while Chris dragged both cases over the threshold.

'Fate,' Chris said whimsically. Maria didn't know if fate had a hand in this, but her heart jigged with renewed excitement. To think Dino must have passed through this very door and along the corridor!

A man passed them pushing a brush along the floor. At her question, he pointed out Dino's dressing room. Chris clasped Maria's hands and squealed. 'Oh, my gosh. We're here!'

Maria knocked on Dino's door,

nerves fluttering in her stomach. When he didn't answer, she rapped again and waited.

'Oh, come on. We're so close. Don't get cold feet now.'

Chris shoved down the door handle and to Maria's surprise it opened. After sharing a wide-eyed glance, they both stared into the small, neat, and very empty dressing room. He wasn't here. But Maria's gaze alighted on something that made her heart bound with joy: Dino's leather jacket hung on a metal railing with some costumes.

Without her making a conscious decision to enter, Maria's feet carried her into the room. She pulled Dino's jacket off the hanger and hugged it, breathing in the fragrance of leather and his oh-so-familiar spicy smell. Tears filled her eyes and all her worries of a moment ago fled. She was here! Soon she would see him, hear his voice, tell him how much she'd missed him. A burst of adrenaline made her giggle crazily, and she danced around the room with his jacket clutched to her chest.

Chris watched from the doorway, her grin fading to a frown. 'You really do love him, don't you?'

Maria stopped and met her sister's gaze. 'Of course. Why would I come all this way otherwise?'

Chris released a heavy sigh. 'I hoped you were just infatuated by the glamour of it all, like me. He's hot, but he's so not right for you, Mari.' She pulled both cases into the room and flopped wearily in an armchair.

Stunned by her sister's comment, Maria plopped onto the upright chair at the dressing table, Dino's jacket clutched possessively in her arms. 'Why did you even come with me if you think that?'

The silence stretched between them for a few minutes.

'I have a confession,' Chris said.

'What?' A shock of foreboding passed through Maria. What had Chris done now?

'I told mum about Dino staying at the Crow's Nest.'

'Christine! Why?'

'She was worried about you. She had some weird idea that Tom had visited and upset you. I don't know where that came from, but I had to tell her the truth.' Chris's breath hissed out between her lips. 'That's why Mum and Dad wouldn't pay your fare to New York.'

'That's so unfair!' Maria cried. 'She doesn't know Dino.'

'She doesn't want to see you hurt, Mari. Neither do I. You hardly said a word to me about Dino after he left Porthale. I thought it was just a holiday romance. Then out of the blue you want to race over here. I thought you were just star-struck and when you got here, you'd realise Dino is not really for you. I came to make sure you had fun anyway.'

Chris's words swirled around Maria's mind. Both Chris and her mum thought she was silly, yearning after a man she could never have. She swivelled her chair away from Chris and stared down at the leather jacket in her hands. She hadn't imagined the time she'd spent with Dino, his affection for her! Even though it felt like a dream sometimes.

'We got on so well,' Maria said softly.

'I know.' Chris leaned over and squeezed Maria's hand. 'But he walked away without leaving you his phone number. When a guy wants to see a girl again, he gives her his number.'

Maria's bubble of euphoria burst and she sagged in her chair. She had told herself this very thing until the postcard arrived.

Maria pressed her fingers to her temples. Sudden weariness throbbed in her head.

'I wish you'd said this before we left home.' Not that it would have stopped her coming, she admitted to herself.

'I'm sorry, Mari. I really am. I like Dino a lot. He's cute and charming. I can totally see why you fell for him, but it was never going to come to anything. I did try to warn you.'

Maria hated when her sister said *I told you so.*

'Do you want to go and find our hotel?' Chris said gently.

'Not yet. Now we're here, I want to talk to Dino. I've come all this way . . . '

Chris shrugged. 'Okay. I just hope he isn't too long. I'm absolutely starving.'

As the minutes ticked past, the last vestige of Maria's hope trickled away and tiredness fell over her like a heavy blanket. Had she really been deceiving herself, as everyone else seemed to think she was?

A noise jerked her head around. A tall blonde woman stood in the doorway. Maria stood slowly, her heart racing. She had seen enough photos and videos of Rachel Tanner to recognise her. In the flesh, she was even more stunning. Reams of thick, honey-blonde hair draped her shoulders, her face perfectly made up, her eyes impossibly blue. She wore a shiny green dress under a fur jacket and Maria suddenly felt dowdy in her jeans and sweatshirt.

A man came through the door behind Rachel and stopped dead. He was older than them, with a touch of grey at his temples, power-dressed in a steel-grey suit. There was a tense moment when they all stared at each other.

The man recovered first and stepped forwards, hand outstretched. 'You must be Maria Gardener. I'm Dino's manager, Freddy Short.'

Maria took his hand cautiously. This was the man who had persuaded Rachel to put Dino's son up for adoption without telling him. He looked like a businessman, but he obviously wasn't trustworthy.

'And you are?' he asked, grasping Chris's hand.

'Maria's sister, Christine.'

'Lovely to meet you, girls.'

'How do you know who I am?' Maria asked.

'I have my sources,' he said with a slick smile. He turned and angled a hand towards the woman. 'This is Rachel Tanner. I'm sure you recognise her from the television.'

'Lovely to meet you,' Chris said, eager to shake Rachel's hand. 'You have a lovely voice. I've listened to all the albums you and Dino have done together.'

'Thank you,' Rachel murmured.

Maria shook Rachel's hand as well and stepped back. Not sure what to say next, she stated the obvious. 'We've come to see Dino.'

'Ah.' Freddy rubbed his hands together. 'That might be a problem. He's very busy for the next few days. It's opening night tomorrow. He's got a press function tonight and Rachel's partnering him. That reminds me.' He turned to the glamorous blonde and rested a hand on her shoulder. 'You'd better head back to the hotel, love, and get ready.'

Rachel gave Freddy a tentative smile,

glanced once more at Maria and left without a word. Freddy watched her go, and then closed the door. His smile dimmed, and his lips tightened.

'I'm sorry you've wasted your time coming all the way out here, love. Dino's got back together with Rachel.'

His words seared through Maria. She caught Chris's sympathetic gaze and tried to mask her hurt and disappointment.

'Dino and Rachel make a great team, Maria,' Freddy Short said gently. 'They work together, socialise together, look good together. They live in the same world. A man like Dino needs a woman who understands the type of pressure and stress he's under with the kind of work he does.'

'Dino sent me a postcard saying he missed me,' she blurted and then realised how pathetic that sounded.

Freddy shrugged. 'It takes at least a week for a letter to make it across the Atlantic. A lot can happen in a week.'

Her heart dropped. Dino had written

the postcard two weeks ago, when he first arrived here. Even if he *had* missed her, then it didn't mean he *still* missed her. He and Rachel had been an item in the past, and everything Freddy said made sense. Were her mum and Chris right? Was she shooting at the moon?

A sigh wrenched at her chest. Perhaps she was being foolish, but she had travelled a long way to see Dino and would not be fobbed off. 'If Dino doesn't have time to see me, I'll understand. But I want to hear it from him.'

'Hadn't you better clean up first? Do something with your hair and put on some make-up?'

Maria glanced in the mirror and ran a hand over her loose hair. It didn't look too bad, but she did look tired. Her skin was pale with dark rings under her eyes, and she felt sweaty and rumpled.

'Look, love. Dino's going to be really tight for time tonight. As soon as he comes out of rehearsals, he'll be dashing off to this press dinner. Go and get some sleep; see him tomorrow when you're feeling fresher.'

'I don't know.' She didn't want to interrupt Dino if he was really busy, but it would only take a moment to say hello and gauge his reaction. 'I'd rather talk to him tonight. He's got to come back here to pick up his jacket. I'll just wait here for him.'

'He isn't coming back.' Freddy grabbed Dino's jacket from her and put it under his arm. 'He asked me to fetch it for him to save time. It's best if you speak to him tomorrow.'

Maria sagged. Her brain felt as if it was full of cotton wool.

'Have you booked a hotel?' Freddy asked.

'Yes.' Chris stepped up beside Maria. 'We're sorted, thanks,' she said.

'Right.' Freddy narrowed his eyes on Chris.

'All we want is a minute of Dino's time,' Chris continued. 'I'm sure he can spare that. We're friends of his.'

'How about I ask him to phone you?' Freddy said. 'Give me your mobile number. He'll call as soon as he gets a moment.'

'How about you give us Dino's number and we'll call him?' Chris retorted.

Freddy's grey eyes homed in on her, cold and serious.

'Look, love, if he'd wanted you to have his mobile number, he'd have given it to you. If he wants to see you, he'll call.'

Maria quickly pulled her phone from her bag and checked it had some charge. She gave Freddy her number and Chris passed over hers as a back-up.

'So Dino will ring tomorrow morning, will he?' Maria asked. 'We're only here for four days.'

Freddy pulled a business card from his pocket and handed it to her. 'Here. If he doesn't call in the next couple of days, let me know and I'll remind him.' He gestured towards the door.

'Shall I see you out?'

'We'll find our own way, thanks.'

Chris and Freddy Short stared each other down for a few seconds, then he turned and walked out.

'What a snake!' Chris cried the moment he was gone. 'I want to see Dino just to tick him off.'

'He's not going to pass on the message, is he?' Maria stared after Dino's manager, feeling defeated.

'Probably not. He doesn't want us seeing Dino for some reason. He was totally freaked out when he saw you.'

Maria's eyes opened wide and she gazed at Chris in surprise. 'Wasn't he just surprised to find us here?'

'It was more than that.' Chris poked her head out the door. 'Quick, he's heading back to the exit. Let's follow him.'

Maria grabbed the handle of her case and followed Chris out. They hurried along the corridor and caught sight of Freddy Short as he neared the stage door. The wheels on the cases hummed on the tiles, so they were hardly stealthy, but he didn't look round. Maria caught the door as it was about to close and they both peeped out to see Freddy climb in a black limousine in the parking area. A moment later it pulled away.

'Blast!' Maria said. If they could have followed, the car might have led to Dino's hotel. 'I wish there was a taxi handy so we could jump in and say 'follow that car' like they do in movies.'

'I thought the same thing.'

Maria and her sister shared a grin, and her mood lifted a little. It would be good to spend time with Chris. They would not let slimy Freddy Short ruin their holiday.

9

The moment the limo door closed, Freddy pulled his phone out. First he keyed in the number for security at the Met and blasted them for allowing the two women access to Dino's dressing room. Something was seriously wrong if any Tom, Dick or Harry could just walk in off the street and get inside.

Seeing the Cornish bird had given Freddy a shock, but it wasn't all bad. He now knew Dino hadn't trusted her with his mobile number. That meant she wasn't important to him. She must have just been in the right place at the right time to offer Dino a little TLC when he needed it. Freddy could relate to that.

He dialled Rachel and tapped his fingers on his knee as he waited for her to pick up. 'Hi, love. You make it back to your hotel okay?' He listened to

Rachel's worries about the press reception and reassured her that she'd be great.

'Listen, love, don't mention anything to Dino about the two women in his dressing room. He needs to focus on his opening night tomorrow, and we've got a big announcement to make after the performance. I don't want to muddy the waters.'

Rachel agreed to keep quiet, as he knew she would.

Freddy slotted his phone back in his pocket and frowned at the crawling traffic. Although he didn't think Maria Gardener posed much of a problem, he wasn't going to risk her getting together with Dino again. He would have her watched, and run interference if necessary.

* * *

Maria woke late the next day and immediately checked her mobile phone. She gave a resigned sigh to see there were no missed calls. The hotel included in their package deal was rather basic and didn't have a restaurant, so she and Chris went to a diner down the street and gorged on fluffy pancakes filled with blueberries and slathered in warm maple butter.

'I vote for shopping!' Chris declared, leafing through a tourist guide of things to do in New York.

Maria wanted to head back to the Met and ask if Dino was there, but he was unlikely to arrive for his evening performance until later in the day. 'Okay, where do you want to go?'

'Fifth Avenue. Check this out.' Chris spread out a map that showed the stores.

'How much have you got to spend?' Maria asked.

Chris dug in her bag and waved her credit card.

'If I let you max that out, Eric will kill me when we get back.'

'I'll just tell him I've bought early birthday presents.'

'Very early! Your birthday isn't for six months.'

Chris simply grinned and gathered her bag and coat. 'Come on. I'm hyperventilating at the thought of new shoes.'

They squeezed between the packed tables and hailed a taxi. It set them down on Fifth Avenue near Central Park.

'Oh my gosh, look, there's Bergdorf Goodman!'

'What do they sell?' Maria asked, turning a circle to take in the wide street and the tall buildings.

'Maria! You're hopeless. Don't you know anything? And why are you wearing those horrible trainers again? I thought they were just for travelling. You can't walk round New York wearing the same clothes you'd hike along the coast path at home in.'

Maria eyed Chris's heels and silently bet herself that by the end of the day, it would be her sister who was bemoaning her choice of footwear.

'I hope we don't get chucked out of the posh shops because you look such a scruff,' Chris continued.

Maria rolled her eyes and hurried after Chris as she took off along the pavement. They wove through the crowd, pausing to admire window displays of clothes and accessories.

'Oh my, I've died and gone to heaven. Look at that — and that!' Chris squealed like a kid in a sweet shop outside Prada and hung on to Maria's arm.

Maria bit her lip and wondered if there was anything in her price range. She would love a new dress and shoes to wear to meet Dino. If she got to see him. She pulled out her phone and checked it was working.

'Have you had any messages?' she asked Chris anxiously.

Her sister checked and shook her head. 'Come on. I want to see as much as I can.'

They went into Juicy Couture and Chris bought a T-shirt. Then they stopped and shared a small gold box of Godiva chocolates.

'Look! There's Saks — we must go in.'

Maria trailed after Chris as she bustled through the metal doors. They headed across the cosmetics section towards the escalator.

'Let's check out the handbags. I need a new one.'

They spent a while examining bags and then moved on to shoes. Chris tried on a few pairs while Maria watched. She was enjoying herself, but in the back of her mind she kept turning over thoughts about Dino.

Even if he was back with Rachel, Maria knew he would not be mean enough to ignore her after she'd come all this way to see him. That meant Freddy hadn't told him she was in New York. She had known he wasn't to be trusted.

She dug in her bag and found Freddy's business card. While Chris paraded around in five inch heels,

Maria rang Freddy's mobile. Her call went through to the answer phone. 'Hi, Freddy, it's Maria Gardener. I haven't heard from Dino yet. If you've forgotten to tell him I'm here, can you do so now and ask him to ring me this afternoon before the opening night, please? I'm only in New York for another two days.'

She ended the call and pushed her phone in her pocket with a sigh. The only way to be certain of seeing Dino was to buy tickets to his performance. At least then she would see him from afar. After the performance, she would try to catch him outside the stage door.

'I'm having these!' Chris sashayed up to where Maria sat, wearing a pair of red shoes with diamante hearts on the front. 'Don't you just love them?'

'They're gorgeous!'

'You try some on.'

Maria kicked off her trainers and tried a few of the pairs Chris had discarded. 'Oh, look at these.' She posed in front of the mirror, angling her foot to see the glittery heel. In the reflection she noticed a bald man watching her from behind a display. As soon as she saw him, his gaze darted away and he moved off. Instinctively Maria clasped her handbag closer.

Maria's pleasure in the shoes disappeared, and she slipped her feet back in her old trainers. 'Pay for your shoes and let's go back to the hotel,' she told Chris.

'Already?' Chris must have seen the discomfort on Maria's face as she didn't argue, simply paid for her purchase and accompanied her out of the store.

Maria kept glancing over her shoulder, looking for the bald guy. They hailed a taxi and it headed to their hotel.

'What was that all about?' Chris demanded, the moment they were safely inside the vehicle.

'There was a man in the shoe department watching me.'

'He probably fancied you.'

'Not that kind of watching. Creepy watching.'

'Are you sure?'

'I think so.'

Chris was thoughtful for a moment. 'I suppose we should be careful. In all big cities you get thieves who prey on tourists.'

They ate a late lunch in the same place they'd had breakfast and headed back to their hotel to change. Maria wore a purple dress and some black heels she borrowed from Chris while her sister matched her new red shoes with a cream skirt and red jacket. 'Don't we look hot!' Chris said twirling in front of the mirror. 'All dressed up for the opera.'

'We haven't got tickets yet.'

'They're bound to have returns. Theatres usually do just before a performance.'

It was after five by the time they left. The temperature had dropped so they wrapped up in coats, scarves and gloves and took a taxi back to the Lincoln Centre.

The sun had started to set and lights

were already popping on across the city. The buildings surrounding the Lincoln Centre plaza glowed, and the fountain was lit from below, the bursts of water sparkling like a fireworks display. Since the previous day, rows of plastic seats had been set up facing the opera house, some already occupied.

Maria headed straight to the Met and passed beneath the arched entrance into the magnificent lobby. An unusual cantilevered staircase curved elegantly up to the next floor, while eleven huge chandeliers hung from the ceiling like starbursts of light. People milled around, laughing and chatting, all wearing evening dress.

'Oh,' Chris looked crestfallen. 'I think we're underdressed.'

'We're fine. Not all the women are wearing long dresses.'

Maria led the way to the box office and joined the queue. When they reached the front, they asked if there were any tickets available. The woman serving gave them an incredulous glance. 'The opening night sold out months ago.'

'What about returns?' Chris retorted.

The woman sighed and tapped on her computer screen. 'A pair of tickets has just become available. I do have a waiting list, but as you're here I'll let you have them.'

'How much are they?'

'Six hundred and seventy-five dollars each.'

'What?' Maria and Chris chorused. The woman couldn't be serious. But her expression said she was.

'That's ridiculous. Our flights cost less,' Chris said.

Maria turned away despondently.

'You can watch outside for free,' a young woman in the queue told her. 'There's a big screen on the front of the building where they show the performance live. If you hurry, you should get a seat.'

'Thank you.' Maria exchanged smiles with the woman and grabbed Chris's hand. 'Come on. Quickly, before the seats fill up.' They darted through the gathering crowd to the doors.

'I wondered what these plastic chairs were for,' Chris said.

'Look up there.' Maria pointed at a huge screen on the front of the Met overlooking the plaza. 'It's not the same as being inside, but it's free.'

And at least she would get to see Dino perform.

They found two seats on the end of a row and while Chris kept their places, Maria bought take-away pizza and a cup of coffee for each of them. They hugged their coats close and munched while the few remaining spaces filled and a crowd collected in the plaza. As people around chatted, Maria felt a flash of pride in Dino every time she heard his name mentioned.

After an hour, the plaza was packed and Chris was shivering. 'I'm not sure I can stick this out. It's so darned cold.'

'Once the performance starts, you'll forget the cold.'

Chris gave Maria a doubtful look.

A cheer went up as the screen finally burst into life. The picture and sound quality were fantastic. Maria's heart leaped when Dino first appeared. She touched the tiny gold heart at her throat and her eyelids fell as memories flooded through her at the first sound of his voice. The songs he sang on the CDs were wonderful, but his voice was so powerful and full of emotion in *La Bohème*. The sound of beauty and emotion, he'd called it that day in the car to Mevagissey — and when he was the one singing, she agreed.

The plot seemed to be a love story that ended with the heroine dying in Dino's embrace. Maria chewed the fingers of her gloves and watched as he held the beautiful, dark-haired actress, wishing that she was the woman in his arms.

The opera ran for nearly three hours. Half way through Chris left to fetch more coffee and didn't return until near the end.

'Sorry I was so long. I sat in the

coffee shop for a while to get warmed up a bit,' she whispered. 'Can we go now?'

'Not until it's finished.' Maria was determined not to miss a moment. After the performance, interviews with the cast were broadcast as they went into a gala dinner. Maria's heart beat faster as Dino appeared on the screen in a midnight-blue dinner jacket and matching bow tie, but her pleasure faded a little to see the ever-present Rachel on his arm, looking incredible in a shimmering, scarlet evening dress.

He graciously accepted praise for his performance and answered questions, his easy smile and enthusiastic manner so familiar that tears pricked Maria's eyes.

'I have an exciting announcement tonight,' he said, grinning. 'I am delighted to have been asked to play Pavarotti in a Hollywood biopic of the great man.'

Spontaneous applause and hoots of approval burst out in the audience.

'Luciano Pavarotti debuted at the Metropolitan Opera as Rudolfo in Puccini's *La Bohème* in 1968. I am deeply honoured to be following in his footsteps.'

The interviewer raved about how awesome it was to be chosen to play such a legend. This was obviously wonderful for Dino's career and tears of joy flooded Maria's eyes to see him so happy, but the tears were bittersweet. As Dino explained they'd be filming in the USA and locations around the world, Maria's spark of hope that she might ever have a place in his life fizzled out.

After his interview, Maria stared blankly at the opera house. She'd been deluding herself. Dino's postcard had probably been a kind gesture, nothing more. She'd been so desperate for a sign of his affection that her imagination had run away with her.

'Maria, can we go now? I can't feel my fingers.'

'I'm sorry, Chris. Come on.'

Maria rubbed her sister's hands, but her own were nearly as chilled. They hailed a taxi and huddled together in the back to get warm as they drove the few blocks to their hotel.

Maria fell into bed, incredibly weary after the shopping and drained from the emotional highs and lows.

'I'm sorry, Mari,' Chris whispered in the dark. 'I know you're upset about Dino. But be happy for him. He's such a sweet guy and this film thing must be a really good thing for him.'

'I know. I am happy. It's just hard.' Maria pressed a hand over her mouth and swallowed back her sadness. She only wanted the best for Dino, but she badly wanted to talk to him just one last time. To wish him luck. To say the goodbye she felt she'd missed out on when he left Cornwall.

The following day Maria persuaded Chris to do some sightseeing. They visited the observatory at the top of the Empire State Building. The city was so vast, so endless. Staring down at the spiky, urban jungle of buildings, Maria longed for the peace and quiet of home, the smell of the salty sea air and the sound of the waves on the beach.

Her phone chimed. Maria checked to find a text from her mum saying she hoped they were having fun. Maria smiled and angled the screen towards Chris.

'I miss the girls,' Chris said wistfully. 'I've enjoyed my break, but I want to go home.'

'Me too.'

Maria had already known she was a homebird like her dad. Her trip to Canada had taught her that, but it was good to be reminded of what was important in life.

She folded her arms on the retaining wall and stared through the safety grid at the tiny cars on the streets far below, her fingertips grazing her gold heart wistfully.

Dino wasn't going to call. Her only chance of seeing him was to wait outside the stage door after his matinée performance the following day. She would just have time before the flight if she and Chris had their bags packed and ready.

* * *

The following morning they took a harbour cruise to see the Statue of Liberty and then headed back to the hotel to collect their cases before eating a late lunch in a restaurant across the road from the Met. They lingered over coffee, people-watching. For a moment, Maria thought she saw the bald-headed man who'd been watching her in Saks, but he climbed into a taxi and she decided she was just being paranoid.

After lunch they wandered around the Lincoln Centre plaza, sat on the side of the waterfall and took photos of each other on their phones as mementoes of the trip.

At three-thirty they headed to the stage door to be sure of a place at the front. As the end of the performance drew near, the crowd swelled. Once the opera finished, more people surged into the corridor, pushing and shoving.

'Holy cow,' Chris said hanging on to Maria's arm with one hand and her case with the other. 'These New Yorkers don't take prisoners.'

As the crowd increased, Maria's hopes faded. Even if Dino saw her, she couldn't say what she wanted to say in front of all these people! Then the doors opened and cast members emerged. Fans elbowed and shoved to get a good view.

'Don't you give up your spot, Mari. Shove back.' Chris pushed Maria forwards and she ducked beneath an arm and around a tall man so she could see. She glanced over her shoulder to see Chris had retreated to the safety of a wall, dragging both cases. Then a cheer went up and everyone clapped. Dino exited the stage door with a hand placed protectively on the back of his beautiful, dark-haired leading lady. They chatted to the crowd and signed autographs while two security guards flanked them.

Maria's pulse raced at the sight on him, his easy smile, warm dark eyes, his oh-so-familiar leather jacket. She shouted his name but it was lost in the noise as other people did the same. She tried to ease closer, but the crowd was packed tight. She wasn't tall enough for him to see her.

She shouted louder, a note of desperation in her voice. His head turned, an arrested look in his eyes, his pen poised over the programme he was about to sign.

'I'm here, Dino!' she shouted and raised her hand to wave. Suddenly a man barged in front of her and she stumbled back, saved from falling only because the people behind were packed so tightly. She rose on tiptoe, but the man who'd pushed in front blocked her view. Frustrated, she shoved him and he cast her a withering glance over his shoulder.

She froze. It was the man from Saks.

She squeaked in fear and shouldered her way back through the throng to Chris.

'What happened?' Chris demanded.

'It's that man, the one who was watching me.' Maria caught sight of his bald head again. 'There!' She pointed.

'Okay. Seriously creepy. I don't like the idea of being down here with him. We need to leave now,' Chris said. 'Here, take your case.'

Dino and his leading lady had moved further down the hall towards their limo and the crowd had gone with them. Chris headed in the other direction.

With a last longing glance over her shoulder, Maria followed.

The sensible thing to do was go home and get on with her life. But she would never forget Dino. Her happy memories of their month together would live on in her heart for the rest of her life.

10

A few days later, Dino was still buzzing from his success at the Met. He loved acting as well as singing. Opera was where his heart lay. He promised himself that at the end of the coming concert tour, he would pursue classical opera full-time and recover his artistic integrity.

The newspapers called him the king of popera, a moniker he'd grown to hate. He hoped it wasn't too late for the hard-core opera community to take him seriously.

He and Rachel passed through security at Toronto airport and headed out to get a taxi.

'Wait a moment, cara,' he said and beckoned Rachel back as he perused the postcards displayed on a tourist stand. He planned to send Maria a card from every city he visited. Even though he had enjoyed his time in New York, Maria was never far from his thoughts.

At the height of his triumph in *La Bohème*, there had still been a small empty place inside him that longed for her. He hadn't known it was possible to miss someone this much, and he wanted to make sure she didn't forget him.

As soon as he had a gap in his schedule, he vowed he would go and visit her.

Rachel looked on moodily while he bought a card and filled out the Crow's Nest address. He didn't hide what he was doing. It was time Rachel knew about Maria and understood that Dino's affections lay elsewhere.

He smiled as he wrote: *In Toronto for the start of my tour. Still missing you! Love Dino.*

'Who's that for?' Rachel asked.

'A woman I met during my month out.' He expected more questions, perhaps a clingy response, but she remained silent. He realised that over the last few days she had been quieter and less demanding of his time. Perhaps she understood that romance between them was off the agenda.

He posted his card and imagined Maria picking it up from the door mat in the Crow's Nest, the look on her face as she read his message. He hoped she would be pleased to hear from him.

Outside the airport, they climbed into a cab and he gave the address of their hotel. He dug out his mobile phone and scrolled through the photographs to find his favourite one of Maria from their day in Mevagissey. His chest ached with longing as he stared at her smiling face, the wind whipping her ponytail up behind her. That had been a good day. One he'd never forget.

He had resisted kissing her. Now he wished he hadn't done the right thing. He wished he had taken every opportunity to kiss her and hold her.

He sucked in a catching breath and released it slowly. Strange that he had to fly half way across the globe before he realised that he loved her.

'Here.' He passed the phone across to Rachel. 'This is Maria, the woman I sent the postcard to.'

Rachel cradled his phone in her hand and stared at the image, biting her lip. A single, silent tear slid down her cheek, and Dino winced. He should have remembered she had feelings for him.

'I'm sorry, cara. Forgive me for being insensitive. I did not mean to upset you.'

More tears spilled down her cheeks, and she pushed the phone back in his hand. 'She was in New York.'

Dino frowned and leaned forwards to see Rachel's averted face. He couldn't have heard her correctly. 'What did you say?'

Rachel turned an anguished expression on him, her lips trembling. 'Don't hate me, Dino.'

'Why would I hate you, cara?'

'Freddy and I found Maria and her sister in your dressing room at the Met.'

Cold trickled through Dino like ice water. 'Maria came to New York? When?'

Rachel sobbed and wiped her eyes. 'The day before you opened in *La Bohème*.'

Dino braced a hand against the door as if he were falling. That was six days ago!

'What happened to her? Where did she go?'

'I don't know. Freddy sent me back to the hotel and told me not to tell you.'

Maria must have felt so lost in New York when she didn't see him, so hurt and disappointed. Thank heavens Chris had been with her. He scraped a hand back through his hair — angry, so angry. 'Did Freddy tell you anything else?'

'He told her you were busy. That's all I know.'

'Is she still in New York?'

Rachel shrugged.

Dino pressed a hand to his forehead, tried to work out if he had time to fly back to New York and still make his performance in Toronto the following night. He had a television interview in a few hours. He could miss that, but he couldn't miss the performance. Ten thousand people had paid for seats, and he would not let them down.

The taxi arrived at the hotel. Dino climbed out and fetched his bag from the boot himself. He paced on ahead of Rachel to the reception desk and checked in, his mind turning over and over, so furious he wanted to shout.

This was the final nail in the coffin. He and Freddy Short were finished. Finito. Done! Dino had intended to let Freddy handle his record deals, but that would not happen now.

He rode up in the elevator, his cheeks hot, his pulse racing. He saw Rachel to her room, then found his own. As soon as the door closed behind him he pulled his phone from his pocket. He dialled Freddy and paced up and down, his fist tight at his side.

Freddy picked up. 'Dino, mate. Are you in Toronto?'

'Why didn't you tell me that Maria

came to see me?'

Silence answered his question. Then he heard Freddy clear his throat. 'I was thinking about your career, Dino. The last thing you need is some lovesick bird tagging around after you.'

Dino rested a hand against the wall and hung his head. When he'd learned about his son he'd felt cold, empty, shocked, but this anger was flaming hot. If Freddy had been there he might have hit him.

'You had no right to interfere,' he grated out between clenched teeth. 'No right. Where is she now?'

'She flew back to London a few days ago.'

Everything inside Dino collapsed like a punctured balloon and he flopped into a chair. She had gone. He hadn't realised how much he'd hoped she was still in North America, still within reach. He rested his forehead in his hand and tried to think.

'Dino, mate,' Freddy said. 'What are you thinking?'

Frustration tightened his muscles. Every time he'd wished Maria was there with him, she could have been. She had been so close, and he hadn't even known.

'Where did she stay?' he demanded, praying that Freddy had looked after her and not abandoned her to fend for herself.

'That sister of hers said they had a hotel booked,' Freddy said defensively. 'I did ask.'

Dino broke the connection and tossed his phone on the bed. He'd thought he heard her voice by the stage door on Saturday but persuaded himself it was wishful thinking. She must have been there in the crowd! He pressed his hand over his eyes.

He felt so helpless. Maria had been hurt — because of him.

* * *

After fifteen hours travelling, Maria and Chris arrived at Truro train station and trudged out, pulling their cases. In all Maria's life she had never felt this tired. Not just physically weary, but mentally and emotionally exhausted.

Eric was parked outside. He climbed out to greet them, pulling Chris into a long hug. 'You didn't run off with an American hunk, then?' he said smiling.

'None of them are as hunky as you, my darling.'

Eric kissed Maria on the cheek and opened the back door for her to climb in while he hefted their suitcases into the boot. Chris hopped in the front and hissed out a huge sigh of relief. 'Am I glad to be home!'

'Yes. Me too.'

And Maria was — even though she had huge challenges to face, namely finding a new job and somewhere to live.

Eric climbed in, started the car and pulled away.

'How are my babies?' Chris asked.

'Tina's babysitting, they're fine, but

they're looking forward to seeing their mum.'

Maria stared out the window at the familiar scenery as Eric negotiated the traffic out of Truro and headed into the country. Although she'd promised herself to be positive, it was difficult. Right now, all she wanted to do was climb into bed, curl into a ball and sleep for a week. But even the Crow's Nest was no longer the sanctuary it had been.

She rested her forehead against the side window and stared blankly outside. Her hopes and dreams for the future were impossible now her parents were selling up, and suddenly the fruitless trip to see Dino felt like the final straw.

Eric turned up the private lane leading to the guesthouse and cut the engine outside the front gate. Maria released a long, pent up-sigh and Chris reached back and squeezed her arm.

'Forget him, Mari. Just forget him. It will hurt for a while, but the pain won't last forever.'

Wiping all memories of Dino from

her mind might be wise, but it just wasn't going to happen. He owned part of her heart.

Her dad hurried down the path, and she climbed out to meet him. 'Good to have you two back safe and sound,' he said, giving her a hug, then leaning in the car to kiss Chris. He lifted Maria's case out and carried it inside.

Maria's mother was waiting at the doorway as she went up the front path. The welcoming smile on her mother's face fell as she watched her approach.

'Oh, dear. What happened, darling?'

She walked into her mum's open arms and wished she was a little girl again, whose hurts could be put right with a cuddle.

'I went all that way and didn't see him.'

Her mother led her through to the kitchen, sat her down and made a cup of tea. 'Tell me what happened,' she said.

The whole sorry tale poured out. Maria told her how Dino had turned up on the doorstep after they left for the cruise, and how she had fallen for him. She ended with a description of the frustrating time in New York.

Her mum sat beside her, gripping her hand. 'Oh, darling, Chris told me it was Dino Rossi you were going to see. I should have warned you not to bother and saved you all this heartache. Men like that aren't interested in girls like you.'

'What's the matter with me?' Maria asked indignantly, even though she knew perfectly well what her mother meant.

'Nothing, darling. Nothing at all. But Dino Rossi lives in a glamorous jet-set world. I'm sure you've read the articles about him on the internet. He has women throwing themselves at him all the time. You don't want to get involved with a man like that.'

'I really liked him, Mum.'

Her mother slid her chair closer and put her arm around Maria's shoulders. 'You'll get over him, just like you did

Tom. The next few years will be exciting for you, darling. You have the world at your fingertips. With no ties, you're free to choose any job you want. Just think about it — with your qualifications, you could work for a tour company anywhere in the world. Isn't that an exciting prospect?'

Maria nodded obediently, even though travelling to another country was the last thing on earth she wanted to do right now.

* * *

Dino was desperate to call Maria, make sure she arrived home safely and explain that he hadn't known she was in New York. He wished he had given her his mobile phone number before he left Cornwall. He couldn't even remember why he hadn't done so.

He calculated the time she would arrive home and rang the Crow's Nest at eight a.m. from Calgary, the next stop on his Canadian tour. He paced nervously back and forth across the hotel room, waiting for the phone to be answered.

'Hello, the Crow's Nest,' a woman's voice said. He guessed it was her mother.

'Hello. I wish to speak with Maria, please.'

Silence.

He rubbed his lips nervously. 'Hello. Are you still there?' he prompted impatiently.

'Yes. Is that Dino?'

He winced at her chilly tone of voice. Of course she would know what had happened to Maria.

'Yes. May I explain please, Mrs Gardener? I did not know that Maria visited New York until after she left.'

She sighed. 'Whether you knew or not is beside the point. Maria was devastated when she arrived home. She's in bed now recovering from jet lag. I'm sure it's hit her extra hard because of the stress. I don't know you, Mr Rossi or Rossellini, or whatever you like to be called, but I do know that this relationship you have with my daughter is bad for her. I don't want you to call her again.'

Dino halted his pacing, heart racing as her words sank in.

'I am very sorry for what happened in New York. I wanted very much to see her.'

Mrs Gardener sighed again, her breath hissing down the phone line.

'Please,' Dino said, 'let me speak to her.'

'No. Maria might be twenty-four, but all the while she's under my roof she's still my little girl. I won't see her hurt like this. Please don't ring again.'

Then the line clicked and the dialling tone sounded in his ear.

Dino stared at his phone with disbelief. Maria's mother had forbidden him from calling as if he were a delinquent teenager! He cursed in Italian and jammed his phone in his pocket. Then he paced angrily in front of the huge picture window, barely noticing the magnificent view of the Rocky Mountains in the distance as his mind raced.

Respect for his elders had been instilled in him at a young age. He would not disobey Mrs Gardener's request, but she had asked him not to phone; she had said nothing about writing.

He sat at the desk in the corner of his room, selected some sheets of hotel paper and poured out his heart. He included his phone number and email address and asked Maria to call him so that he could arrange to see her again. Then he sealed the envelope and prayed she would forgive him for hurting her.

*   *   *

Maria spent a week recovering from her trip to New York. Then she made herself a promise; she would not mope around and feel sorry for herself. She needed to take control of her life, find a job and create her own future.

She tried not to think of Dino, but she still rushed downstairs every morning to check for another postcard. When her mother assured her that no postcards had arrived, she had to accept that the New York card must have been a one-off he'd sent simply on a whim.

After she realised this, she resisted searching his name online every day to follow the news about his tour. Instead she used the internet to search for jobs. She made a few appointments, requested application forms and got a lucky break when she rang a new spa hotel only eight miles away that was looking for an assistant manager. The man they had appointed let them down at the last minute so they needed to replace him quickly.

Ten days after she had arrived back from New York, she drove down the country lanes to the Eden Bach Hotel and Spa. She turned between tall granite pillars and followed the private drive through beautifully maintained gardens, bright with the colour of primroses, crocuses and daffodils, to a manor house.

Maria parked and made her way into the building. The entrance hall had been converted into a tasteful lobby with a reception desk along one side manned by two staff members. She approached the nearest receptionist and smiled.

'Maria Gardener for Mr Calder.'

'Take a seat, please. I'll let him know you're here.'

A few minutes later, a nice-looking man with brown hair and grey-blue eyes emerged from a door nearby and held out his hand in greeting. 'Miss Gardener, good of you to come at such short notice.' He had a firm handshake and a pleasant manner. She simmered inside with hope and expectation. This could be the answer to her prayers. A place where she would enjoy working, not far from her family.

Mr Calder ushered her into his office and directed her to a chair. 'I've reviewed your CV, and I can't fault your qualifications or experience. We're all about customer service here. The Eden Bach group prides itself on providing the personal touch. Every guest must feel as though they are the most important person in the hotel, and your philosophy on customer service gels nicely with that. In fact, you could have written our mission statement.' He laughed and Maria smiled with him.

They discussed the hotel and the opportunity for promotion. The good feeling she'd had when she arrived had grown into a certainty that this hotel chain was different, in a positive way.

'I like the sound of everything you've said so far. I definitely feel Eden Bach is a company I would be happy working for.'

'Let me get someone to show you round properly, Miss Gardener, then come back and see me in thirty minutes and we'll discuss the details.'

Did that mean she had the job? Maria's heart bounded as Mr Calder summoned a receptionist to be her guide. Everything about the place was top quality. She even liked the staff uniform; a classy burgundy blazer and navy skirt.

Maybe getting out into the world was a good thing. She would meet single men, and she might find one she wanted to marry. Perhaps her dream of marrying and running a guesthouse with her husband was not impossible after all.

In the midst of her enthusiasm, an unwanted memory of Dino sneaked into her mind. Her heart hadn't caught up with the reality that Dino was gone forever — but it would. One day.

'Very impressive,' she said, as Mr Calder ushered her back in his office.

'That's what I like to hear.' He indicated that she should sit down and tapped his fingers on some forms. 'I took the liberty of ringing our head office to confirm your appointment. If you want it, the job's yours.'

'Oh!' Maria's hand flew to her heart.

She liked the place, could imagine working here, but still . . . It took her a moment to gather her thoughts. 'I thought I'd be sitting by the phone for a week before I heard.'

'We need someone quickly. There's a company induction course running next week. That will be the last one for a while. I'd like you to be on it if you're going to join us.'

'Next week!' Everything was happening so fast. 'Where would I have to go?'

'They take place at the head office in London.'

Maria bit her lip, her pulse racing. She had no reason to turn down such a good job, except for her own resistance to change. She smiled and nodded.

'Yes, Mr Calder, I accept,' she said quickly, before she had time to change her mind. 'I think I'll enjoy working here.'

'Great! That's settled, then. I'll get the official letter in the post to you today. The training course starts at ten-thirty on Monday morning at the

Eden Bach Hotel in Mayfair, the chain's flagship hotel overlooking Hyde Park.'

Maria's head was spinning. She had a new job. No; this change was more fundamental than that. She had a new life.

11

The following Monday, Maria strode out of the Eden Bach hotel in Mayfair, and stared longingly across six lanes of traffic at the green oasis of Hyde Park. She had come up by train the previous evening and spent a nervous night in the luxury hotel. But everyone was friendly and the first morning of her training course had gone well.

She found a deli, bought a sandwich and coffee, and waited at traffic lights to cross Park Lane. A red double-decker bus pulled up, its brakes squealing, and Maria's heart faltered at the advertisement plastered across its side. *DINO ROSSI LIVE AT THE 02 ARENA.* Dino and Rachel stood together, an orchestra behind them, surrounded by a glittering border of red and gold.

Maria stared dumbstruck as the bus

moved away. Sweat prickled her skin as heat flushed through her. The lights changed, and someone shoved her in the back, grumbling to make her hurry. Thoughts swirled as she dashed across the road with the crowd and stumbled through the gate into Hyde Park, breathless.

She found a vacant bench and dropped down, her sandwich forgotten. Dino was performing in London on the last day of her course! She gripped the small gold heart still hanging around her neck. She could go to watch him live!

No. This was crazy. What happened to her promise to move on? But the memories and longings assailed her as strongly and as deeply as ever.

Maria checked her watch. She had only a few minutes to return to the meeting room. Flustered, she tossed her sandwich in a bin and hurried back. As the course tutor droned on about customer service principles, Maria's thoughts were all of Dino. She barely heard a word of the presentation.

As soon as the class ended, she hurried to her room, used her new company laptop to search the internet for ticket agencies and booked a seat for Dino's performance.

The rest of the course passed in a blur. By the end of the week, she could hardly sit still with excitement and nerves over seeing Dino. Her new job felt like an irritation. She wanted the course to just hurry up and finish.

When the evening of the concert finally arrived, Maria changed into jeans and caught the Underground to North Greenwich. It was only a short walk from the station to the 02 Arena and she didn't have any difficulty finding her way. Everyone seemed to be walking in the same direction. The roof of the arena soared high into the night sky, a huge dome speared with glowing metal spikes. The place resembled a flying saucer perched on the edge of the River Thames.

In the midst of the crowd, she was

swept up to the gates and through the door into the building, past the shops and up an escalator to her seat. The inside of the place was huge, like a football stadium, with rows and rows of seats, holding nearly twenty thousand people. She sat down and hugged her coat around her as others seated themselves. All these people had come to see Dino . . . her Dino. The man who had danced her around the Crow's Nest kitchen, held her in his arms.

She was so far from the main stage that she had to squint to see the orchestra taking their places. Multi-coloured lights strobed over the crowd, flickering and flashing like fireworks. The chatter of expectant voices filled the arena. Seats rattled and footsteps thumped on the steps as the last people hurried to their places.

The orchestra struck up. Every muscle in Maria's body was strung tight, her palms damp.

Then Dino strode out from the side

of the stage, confident, smiling. Deafening applause rose from the crowd. Maria wouldn't have been able to see him clearly, but for a huge LCD screen behind the orchestra that showed him in close-up. He grabbed a microphone from a stand and raised his arms for silence. The clapping faded.

'Buona sera! Good evening, London,' Dino said. 'How are you tonight?'

The crowd cheered again, but Maria stared mutely, her throat tight with emotion. She felt as though she had slipped into an alternative reality. The otherworldly feeling continued as Dino glanced at the conductor and nodded.

The first song was in Italian. Because she didn't understand the words, she concentrated on the beautiful intonation of his voice, memorising each note, each gesture, desperate to remember. Much as she had enjoyed hearing him sing *La Bohème,* these popular songs were the style of music she enjoyed most.

Sometimes he paused his singing and

danced a few bars, his elegant, fluid movements so achingly familiar that tears ran down Maria's cheeks. Watching him live was a very different experience to seeing him on the screen in New York.

This was exquisite torture, as painful as a blade sliding silently into her heart. She shouldn't have come. What had she been thinking?

Between songs, he talked to the crowd, mentioned other places he'd performed, joked about things that had happened. He had such charisma that the audience hung on his every word. How could she ever have thought in her wildest dreams that he would want her? Her mum had been right. She had been deluding herself.

She wiped her tears and told herself to leave, but she couldn't drag her hungry eyes from Dino. This must be the last time she'd see him. Her heart couldn't stand it again.

Rachel sashayed on stage in a gold satin dress and sang three songs with

Dino. Flickering lights danced over the eager upturned faces of the audience as Dino and Rachel held hands, stared into each other's eyes and sang of love lost and found.

The crowd erupted into ecstatic applause at the end. Grinning, Dino kissed Rachel's hand, in just the same way as he had once kissed Maria's.

Maria buried her face against her sleeve as the adulation continued. She couldn't take much more of this. The clapping seemed to go on forever.

When Maria finally raised her gaze, Dino and Rachel had left the stage, but the orchestra was still there.

The audience continued to clap, people drumming their feet on the floor, cheering for an encore. Part of Maria hoped that Dino wouldn't answer the call; that this was the end, and she could escape to lick her wounds, but her stupid heart still ached for one last sight of him.

After what felt like an eternity, Dino ran on stage again and picked up the microphone. This time he was alone. 'Ah, you Londoners, you are too demanding.' He gestured in a familiar way. Then his smile faded, and he glanced down thoughtfully.

'Now I will sing something that is special to me.' As he spoke, he moved away from the orchestra, along an elevated walkway to a small stage in the centre of the arena. The circular platform raised Dino ten feet high, and the eager faces of his fans stared up at him.

Coloured lights flickered over the crowd and the orchestra started playing softly. 'A little while ago I met a woman,' Dino said, his words echoing around the arena. He kissed the tips of his fingers and held them up, releasing the kiss into the air. 'This song is for her.'

Like everyone else in the arena, Maria was transfixed. A spotlight illuminated Dino from above, shining off his glossy dark hair, making him look almost surreal. Then he started singing, and Maria forgot to breathe.

She recognised the song immediately — *Maria* from *West Side Story*. She clamped a hand over her mouth and tears spilled from her eyes as he sang her name, over and over, his voice laden with emotion. This song must be for her. Even as her mind rejected the idea, her heart knew it was true.

If he felt this way about her, then why hadn't he contacted her? Not a phone call or a postcard since she came back from New York. Nothing to keep her hopes alive. It made no sense.

And how could she ever get in touch with him to let him know she felt the same way?

★　★　★

Maria caught an early-morning train home the following day. She watched the London suburbs slip past, gradually giving way to fields and villages. Her mum and dad had invited her grand-parents over for dinner that evening to celebrate Maria's new job. She tried to think of the family celebration she was returning to, the food she would prepare, but Dino completely filled her thoughts.

His rendition of *Maria* had left her more confused than ever. Why sing a song for her when he had no idea she was in the audience? Had it simply been a sentimental crowd-pleaser to end the performance? She didn't want to believe he was insincere, but if the sentiments he expressed in the song were true, surely he would have found time to stick a stamp on a postcard and send it her way?

This whole situation with Dino exhausted her — the emotional highs and lows, the uncertainty, the heartache. She should have stuck to her plan to put him behind her and move on. Then she remembered the agony of emotion on his face as he'd sung her name, and she knew that memory would remain with her until her dying day.

Four hours later, when she walked out of Truro station, she saw her sister's car parked in one of the pick-up bays. As soon as Chris spotted Maria, she jumped out. 'Hiya. You've got me! Mum and Dad have had a few viewings and they're showing another couple round the guesthouse.'

Maria's heart fell. She'd managed to put the sale out of her mind for the last week.

'Why today, when we've got a family do?'

'It was the only time they could manage.' Chris hauled Maria's case into the back of her vehicle.

They set off, and Chris quizzed Maria on her course and listened with rapt attention to the details of the posh London Eden Bach hotel.

'You are so lucky. I'd love a shopping trip to London.'

Maria laughed. 'Has your credit card recovered from New York? Anyway, I wasn't shopping. I was on a training course.'

'In one of the classiest hotels in London.' Chris released a heartfelt sigh. 'But I can't complain. I've got a good life.'

'You certainly have — a husband who loves you and two lovely little girls.' It was Maria's turn to sigh. Chris had everything Maria wanted.

'So if you had such a good time, why do you look like a wet weekend?' she asked bluntly.

'I do not.' Maria pulled down the sun visor and examined her face in the mirror. She did look a bit pale. She planned to tell her sister that the traffic noise had disturbed her sleep, but when she opened her mouth, different words came out.

'Dino was on at the 02 Arena last night.'

'Oh, Mari. Please tell me you didn't go.'

Maria winced.

'Didn't you learn your lesson in New York?' Her sister gave her an exasperated glance, but after a few moments she relented. 'Okay, spill. What was the concert like?'

Maria described the venue and the songs Dino had performed, but she didn't mention the encore. Although he'd sung *Maria* in front of twenty thousand people, the experience was too personal to discuss.

As soon as she arrived home, her mother recruited her for kitchen duty. 'Granny and Grandpa will be here soon and they're staying tonight. I know it's crazy, but there's snow forecast. I can't understand what's happened to the British weather. We never used to get much snow in the South West, and certainly not at this time of year. I don't know what's happened to the global warming they promised us. It feels more like a new ice age sometimes.'

Maria set to baking rolls and preparing vegetables. The pleasure of being in the kitchen and cooking soothed her fraught emotions. Her one regret about joining Eden Bach was that she'd no longer cook for guests.

She would have to satisfy her culinary urges by cooking for her family.

For once, the weather forecast was right and by mid-afternoon fluffy snowflakes had started to fall. Her father's parents arrived soon afterwards, and she took a break from the kitchen to welcome them.

Grandma Gardener was a fraction over five feet tall, but rather like a feisty small dog, she had the attitude of a Rottweiler.

'Let me look at you.' She patted Maria's cheek. 'Hmm, you're too pale and too thin, but I expect that's the fashion these days.' Maria smiled as she gave her granny a hug. 'What's this new job you've got then, poppet? I want to hear all about it.'

Over a cup of tea, Maria gave a brief rundown of her assistant manager's job to everyone there and hoped she wouldn't be asked that question again. Although they were here celebrating her new job, she didn't want to spend the weekend thinking about work.

'Well, I hope you enjoy it,' Granny commented. 'It doesn't seem right to me, your mum and dad selling the guesthouse out from under you when you've worked so hard here.'

'We've talked about this, Mum,' Maria's dad said, tapping a finger against his lips for silence.

'Yes, well, I'm just saying, that's all. I'm allowed to have an opinion, aren't I?'

Maria squeezed her granny's arm, grateful for the support, even though she knew the Crow's Nest issue was a lost cause.

At five-thirty Maria and her mother wheeled the heated trolley into the dining room and served the dinner. Including Chris, Eric and the twins, there were nine of them and to accommodate them, most of the tables had been moved aside, leaving three pushed together in the centre of the room.

Maria paused for a moment and, with a pang of longing, remembered the last time she had eaten in the dining room — with Dino. She remembered the sound of his laughter and his soft, melodic accent, the glint of warmth in his rich, brown eyes.

That felt like a lifetime ago now.

'We arrived just in time. Look at the snow falling.' Granny pointed her walking stick at the bay window overlooking the village. 'That'll put paid to all those poor daffodils that dared pop up their heads early.' She patted Maria's arm. 'Come and sit beside me, poppet.'

Maria pulled out a chair and helped the old woman to settle. She and her mother placed the dishes of vegetables on the table and handed out servings of steaming, fragrant roast lamb.

Chris cut up Charlotte's and Poppy's meat, then served them with vegetables. The two little girls started shovelling the food into their mouths on plastic spoons.

'Don't you feed those girls at home, Christine?' Granny asked, winking at Maria.

Chris simply rolled her eyes and ignored the dig.

Once everyone had been served Maria finally sat down and spooned vegetables onto her own plate. She had just taken her first mouthful when the doorbell chimed.

'Oh, for goodness' sake,' her mother exclaimed. 'Why does that always happen the minute I sit down?'

Maria started to get up, but Chris was already on her feet moving towards the door. Maria turned to chat to her dad, who was certain that the people who had viewed the guesthouse that morning would make an offer. Maria secretly hoped they wouldn't. She knew the place had to be sold, but she didn't want to start flat-hunting until she had settled into her new job.

Chris's heels clicked on the parquet floor as she paced back into the dining room, a huge grin on her face.

Then Maria noticed a man behind her. A dark-haired man.

Maria's heart faltered. Her breath

caught in her lungs. Dino followed Chris into the dining room and halted just inside the door. Silence fell as everyone looked up.

Dino's gaze swept the table and settled on her — dark, intense, uncertain. Oblivious to everything else, Maria stared back, drank in every detail of him. Specks of snow glittered in his black hair like stars in the night sky; streaks of colour from the cold ran along his cheekbones. A luxurious chestnut fur coat enveloped him, the collar turned up against the chill.

He'd come back to her! In an instant, the disappointment of New York and all the weeks of separation and heartache melted away as if they were a bad dream.

Dino's lips curved in a tentative smile, and nerves tingled to life all through Maria's body as if she had been half asleep since he left. In her fantasies, when they met again she ran into his arms and kissed him, but she could hardly throw herself at him in front of her family.

Belatedly she remembered her manners. She stood and went to him, brushing her fingertips across his soft fur sleeve.

'Mum, Dad, this is my friend Dino Rossellini.'

'Mr Gardener, Mrs Gardener,' Dino said in his beautiful accented English. He stepped forwards as her father stood and shook his hand. 'Forgive me for disturbing your dinner, sir. I would like to speak to Maria, if I may.'

Maria pressed a palm over her heart, feeling almost lightheaded. This was her Dino. How could he be the same man she'd watched singing to thousands of people mere hours ago?

'You'd better stay to dinner,' Maria's mother said, jumping up and bustling around, fetching another place setting and making room on the table.

'Thank you, Mrs Gardener. That is very kind of you, but I cannot stay long.'

Maria's euphoria faded at his words.

Of course — this was a flying visit before he jetted off to his next concert venue.

Despite his comment, Dino took off his coat and sat obediently when Maria's mother indicated a chair.

'Sit down, Mari, and finish your dinner,' her mother said tersely. Maria hesitated behind Dino, longing to touch him. Instead she returned to her seat.

His gaze rose to find Maria's again as he was given a plate and served with vegetables. All she wanted to do was sneak away somewhere private with him.

She had so many questions, she didn't know where to start.

When her mother sat down with a harassed sigh, Maria noticed that she didn't look as impressed with Dino as everyone else did.

Maria tried to continue her meal, but her mouth was so dry she could barely swallow. In the end she gave up trying.

As soon as Dino finished eating, Maria stood up. 'Excuse us for a few minutes. If Dino's short of time, I don't want to hold him up any longer.'

Heart racing, she led him through to the conservatory where they had spent many evenings together, staring up at the stars and talking. Her neck prickled at the firm tread of his footsteps following her across the mosaic tiles of the hallway. Her cheeks were flushed by the time she reached the conservatory and turned to face him. He was wearing a smart dark suit, but his shirt was open at the neck as though he'd taken off his tie.

He took her hands, lifted them to his mouth and kissed her knuckles. 'Maria, Maria, amore mio.' Dino pressed his lips to the backs of her hands again and closed his eyes for a moment. 'I have so much to apologise for. I don't know where to begin.'

She'd assumed he didn't know about her trip to New York, but his words changed her mind. Yet he hadn't contacted her until now. Her bruised feelings welled up, and she pulled her hands out of his grip.

'You left without saying goodbye.'

'Oh, cara. I thought I was doing the right thing.' He gestured in frustration. 'This has not gone well between us since I left. I'm sorry. I did not learn you were in New York until you had gone. Rachel told me when we arrived in Toronto.'

'So why didn't you call me? You could have found the guesthouse phone number on the internet.'

Dino passed a hand over his face, his expression pained. 'It is difficult to say, Maria. I did not want to cause more problems between us.'

'What problems could you possibly have caused by phoning me?' She had no doubt at all that she loved this man and he must have feelings for her — or he wouldn't have travelled down here to see her, but he had a very funny way of showing it.

'Will you forgive me, Maria? Give me another chance.'

'Oh, Dino . . . ' Maria dropped into

one of the wicker chairs and rested her face in her hands. 'I don't blame you for not seeing me in New York. That was Freddy Short's doing. But it made me realise that you and I live different lives. We think differently, have different priorities.'

Dino crouched in front of her and stroked the hair back off her face. 'We are not so different, cara. Don't you remember our time together here?'

'But that wasn't real life for you, Dino. I saw what your life is like when I came to New York. I watched *La Bohème* on the screen outside the Met. I heard about the film you're doing. I was outside the stage door after your matinée performance.'

'Maria, amore, I thought I heard your voice then. Why did you not come to me? I would have been overjoyed to see you.'

Maria remembered the shoving crowd, the bald man who had pushed in front of her. She had forgotten about him once she arrived home, but now she realised he must have been following her if she'd seen him three times in as many days.

'I think there was a man watching me to make sure I didn't get close to you . . .'

'Freddy!' A string of Italian words slid from Dino's lips and she guessed it was a good thing she couldn't understand them. 'He is despicable, but he will not interfere between us again. I have thrown him in the toilet.'

A giggle burst from Maria. 'I don't think that's quite what you mean, Dino. But I understand the sentiment.'

Her flare of amusement abated and she smoothed a hand across his shoulder and touched his hair to reassure herself he was real.

'Dino, I'm over the moon to see you, but why did you leave it so long to contact me? I've really missed you. I'd have loved to hear your voice and know you hadn't forgotten me.'

He sighed softly and ran his fingers across her cheek. 'I did call, you, cara.

Your mother, she told me not to ring again. I hoped you would accept my letter as apology.'

Maria's heart jumped with a painful clench. 'Mum told you not to ring? And you sent me a letter? What letter?'

'I wrote to you as soon as I realised I could not speak to you on the phone. You should have received it by now.'

'I didn't get your letter.' Their eyes met and a moment of understanding passed between them. Maria groaned.

'Mum,' she said, her throat so tight with emotion that the word was barely a whisper.

'Did you not get the postcards I sent you?' Dino continued.

Maria shook her head slowly. Her mother must have checked the post and hidden any mail from Dino.

'She told me you were the wrong sort of man for me.'

'She probably thought she was protecting you, cara.'

Maria closed her eyes until she could get her emotions under control. She had no doubt that her mother's actions had been well-intentioned — but instead of protecting her from hurt, she had succeeded only in causing her several weeks of unnecessary, bitter heartache.

'In my letter, I gave you my phone number and asked you to call me. I wanted to arrange for you to come to Italy with me for my mamma's fiftieth birthday. When I did not hear, I thought you were angry with me and would not see me again, but I could not give up without hearing you speak the words.'

'Oh, Dino!' Maria wrapped her arms around his neck and pressed her face against his hair as he enveloped her in his embrace. They held each other for long minutes, then Dino eased back and cupped her cheek in his palm.

'I don't have long, cara. I must leave soon or I will miss my flight home. I want you to meet my family and see where I grew up. Will you come with me?'

Maria leaned her forehead on his shoulder. She desperately wanted to go, and the thought of refusing and hurting his feelings was awful, but every moment she spent with him would make it harder to part again.

'You'll have to go away to start filming soon. It'll tie you up for months, won't it?'

'Maria, amore.' He raised her hand to his lips again, the look in his brown eyes so loving and earnest. 'Do not worry about that now. Please, come home with me. It is just a week in Italy.'

Doubt flooded her mind. What about her new job, her family, her new life? But they faded as she realised she would never forgive herself if she didn't grab this opportunity. If she didn't go now, she might never know if they stood a chance.

'Yes,' she whispered. 'I'll come.'

12

Maria squinted through the windscreen as Dino drove up the narrow lane out of Porthale. He had hired a four-wheel drive vehicle, which was a good thing as snow was pelting down. It probably wouldn't settle for long at this time of year, but right now the steep hill out of the village would be too slippery to navigate in a normal car.

In the darkness she could barely see Dino, but she stared at his profile, still finding it hard to believe that he had come back to find her. They headed to Newquay airport for a connecting flight to Bristol. From there they would fly to Pisa in Italy. Her hastily packed bag was in the boot, and she hoped that she hadn't forgotten anything. It had been difficult to concentrate on packing with her mother pleading with her to think again.

She knew her mother was being cautious because she didn't want to see her hurt, but when she had grudgingly handed over to Maria the pile of postcards and the letter from Dino, Maria had been obliged to bite her tongue to hold back words she would regret.

The snow was lighter near the north coast of Cornwall, so Newquay airport was open. Dino checked his watch before he lifted her bag from the car. 'We should be in time for our flight from Bristol as long as we hurry.'

He locked the vehicle, took her hand, and they dashed across the car park towards the terminal building. Dino halted inside the doors, pulled some sunglasses from his pocket and slipped them on.

Maria raised her eyebrows in surprise. 'Dino, it's dark. What are you doing?'

'I do not want people to recognise me,' he muttered.

An incredulous chuckle burst from

Maria's lips. With snow glittering on his black hair and the fur coat, he looked as though he had just stepped off a magazine cover. The few people nearby were already ogling him in fascination. They might not know who he was, but it was obvious that he was somebody. He had a personal magnetism that made him stand out in any situation no matter what he wore.

'The dark glasses are not going to work, believe me,' she said. 'And the fur coat is a bit of an attention-grabber.'

He looked down at himself as he put the glasses away.

'It is not real fur, cara.'

At his bemused look, she kissed his cheek. He really had no idea how gorgeous he was.

'You're missing the point, Dino.'

He smiled and held her close for a moment.

'I will miss it more often if it makes you kiss me. Anyway, I do not have a problem in England, usually. The

British are polite. They do not accost me.'

'What about the Italians?' she asked as Dino took her hand and they headed across the terminal building.

Dino laughed. 'The Italians, they ignore me. They like to show me I am nothing special. It is the Americans who mob me.'

They bypassed the check-in desk and Maria frowned.

'Don't we need to drop off my bag?'

'No, cara. Your bag comes with us.'

Dino left her for a moment and spoke to someone in uniform. Then he returned and led her along a corridor to a door that was unlocked by a security guard.

'Where are you taking me?'

He grinned at her. 'Be patient. You will see.'

They emerged onto the concourse and found a vehicle waiting for them. After they piled in, it headed across the runway. Floodlights picked up a helicopter parked in an area set off to the side of the main airport.

'That's for us?' Maria gasped.

'It was the only way. I had an important interview at lunchtime, which is why I could not leave London any earlier. But I must arrive home tonight. Mamma has arranged a big dinner in honour of my visit so I cannot miss it.'

He'd gone to all this trouble on the offchance that she would come with him? However much had the helicopter cost?

Before she had time to dwell on it, they pulled up and Dino handed her out of the vehicle. A man in orange coveralls loaded her case into the helicopter and Dino helped her climb in. She settled in the seat, staring around curiously. This was a first for her. Dino chatted with the pilot who had brought him down from London. Then the engine started and the rotor blades whirred so loudly that they had to shout to communicate.

The pilot checked that they were

both strapped in, spoke on his headset and about ten minutes later they lifted into the sky. Maria laughed with exhilaration and clutched Dino's hand as the aircraft rose and she watched as tiny white snowflakes splattered the glass windows.

Once they gained height and headed off, Dino leaned closer and put his mouth to her ear. 'I have been dreaming of arriving home with you by my side.'

Her heart fluttered at his words. He did manage to say all the right things, but then he was Italian and they were notoriously romantic!

They arrived at Bristol airport in time to catch their flight to Pisa. After a pleasant flight spent chatting and catching up, they landed in Italy and collected their bags.

Hand in hand, they walked out to be met by Dino's brother. The man who greeted them looked like an older version of Dino. He smiled as they approached and pulled Dino into a bear hug, kissing both his cheeks. They chatted in Italian, their voices rising and falling with excitement at seeing each other again.

Then Dino put his arm around Maria's shoulders and gently led her forward.

'Rob, this is my friend, Maria. Maria, this is my eldest brother, Roberto. He is the one who owns the fish restaurant.'

'Maria, it is good to meet you.' Roberto shook her hand, grinning. Then his gaze moved to Dino and he laughed.

'Ah, Mamma will not be happy with you, Dino.'

'Is there something wrong?' Maria demanded with sudden anxiety, sensing that his comment somehow related to her.

Roberto ruffled Dino's hair. 'My little brother did not tell his mamma he was bringing a girlfriend home for dinner.'

'It is all right, Maria. Do not worry.' Dino pulled out his phone. 'I will call her now. She will be pleased to see you.

I did not want to jinx my chance of persuading you to come by telling Mamma to expect you.'

Dino talked on his phone while they walked through the airport, gesturing with emotion as he spoke. Roberto pushed the luggage cart carrying their cases.

'Is everything all right?' Maria demanded as soon as Dino got off the phone.

'Of course. Take no notice of Rob. He likes to tease me. Mamma is delighted that you have come.'

The drive to Riomaggiore seemed to take forever. They had landed in Pisa just before ten in the evening and Maria couldn't imagine how they would arrive in time for the big family dinner Dino had mentioned.

She sat in the front of a van emblazoned *Ristorante Rossellini*, sandwiched between Dino and Rob. The temperature was much warmer in Italy than England and made her drowsy. She nodded off, and woke as they arrived, with her head nestled against Dino's shoulder.

He smiled down at her as she climbed out a little uncertainly. 'Welcome to Riomaggiore, Maria. Welcome to my home town.'

The houses were tall and narrow, streaks of light shining through the gaps in shuttered windows. They'd parked in the steep main street outside Rob's restaurant.

Dino took her hand while Rob carried her bag and led them along a covered walkway and down some old stone steps.

'This is the only way through to the harbour,' Dino said. 'No motor vehicles can reach it.'

Pretty, narrow houses balanced precariously on the steep cliffs surrounding the small bay, the few windows not masked by shutters glowing with warm light. The Rossellini house was one of those closest to the harbour. Wooden boats were pulled up on the cobbles in front of the building. She remembered the village from the picture Dino had shown her on his phone weeks ago.

Although the place was quite different to Porthale, the fishy smell and gentle hiss of the sea reminded her of home.

'My mother and father cannot speak English, cara, but the rest of my family all speak some. One of us will translate for you if necessary,' Dino assured her.

Maria pulled out the tie holding her ponytail and refastened it to make sure her hair was neat, and to give her a moment's breathing space before they went inside.

After weeks of hearing nothing from Dino, she was about to be welcomed by his family. Suddenly everything seemed to be happening very fast and she wasn't sure she was ready.

Rob took care of Maria's case while Dino led her into a terracotta-tiled entrance hall. He tossed his fur coat over the newel post at the bottom of the stairs and ushered her along a narrow passage to the back of the house. The mouthwatering smell of cooking filled her nostrils. They mounted five steps

284

and went through a door into the kitchen.

The chatter of voices almost overwhelmed her as she entered. There were so many people — young, old and in between — crowded into every spot where it was possible to sit. A shared exclamation of pleasure burst out at the sight of Dino.

'Give me a moment, cara,' he said and went in. Maria waited in the doorway as his family leapt to their feet and surrounded him, all talking at once, the hugging and kissing interspersed with affectionate slaps on the back.

A middle-aged woman wearing an apron came forwards with her hands raised and he lifted her off her feet as he hugged her. When he returned her to the ground, she patted his cheek, tears in her eyes. 'Ah, Dino, chicco . . . '

They spoke so fast that Maria was sure she wouldn't be able to keep up with the conversation even if she had been able to speak Italian, but she heard Dino mention her name, then he put his arm around her and escorted her into the melée.

'Hello, Maria Gardener,' the woman he'd hugged said warmly. 'Buona sera.'

'My mother says good evening,' Dino explained. 'My father is over there.' He indicated a grey-haired man asleep in an armchair. 'I will introduce you to him later in the evening.'

'Buona sera, Mrs Rossellini,' Maria said, hoping she had the pronunciation right.

Rob came in and further 'ciaos' erupted as everyone headed for a huge table to one side of the kitchen. From the front the house appeared tall and narrow, but at the back it opened out to twice the width, obviously having been extended behind a neighbouring property.

Maria was squeezed in beside Dino. After he introduced her to most of the people around the table, including his eight nieces and nephews, the beautiful young woman on Maria's other side introduced herself.

'I'm Giuliana,' she said. 'Dino's younger sister.'

'Your English is good,' Maria replied. Giuliana had less of an accent than Dino.

'I study English and politics at Rome University.'

'Giuliana wants to be an anarchist,' Rob said from across the table. She snapped something at him in rapid Italian, earning a stern look from her father.

'They do not understand that I have ambitions. Mamma and Papa think I should want nothing more than to marry, pop out babies and cook.' She made a rude sound and tossed back a glass of wine in a couple of swallows.

'Maria is a culinary angel,' Dino said. 'She cooks the best food I have ever tasted — except for Mamma's, of course.'

Dino repeated his words in Italian, covered her hand with his and smiled. The babble of conversation lulled and all heads turned her way. Heat flooded

287

Maria's cheeks as she realised she would have to say something.

'I know it's not for everyone, especially these days, but I do love cooking,' she said shyly. 'And actually, my dream has always been to have lots of children — then I will cook for them.'

Mrs Rossellini and Giuliana exchanged a few words in Italian, then Giuliana smiled at Maria and translated for her, 'Mamma was worried that Dino would marry Rachel Tanner — but now that he has you by his side to care for him, she is happy.'

By his side to care for him? Maria laughed nervously. What did that mean?

She cast a questioning glance at Dino, only to find him laughing along with the others.

'Ignore them, cara. Mamma has been trying to marry me off ever since I left home many years ago. She thinks that I need looking after.'

★ ★ ★

The clock on the wall said it was nearly one-thirty in the morning, but the Rossellini family were still bright and chatty. Even the children were still going strong. Maria was glad that she hadn't eaten much earlier as she was served a selection of pasta and fish dishes followed by delicious fruit-filled bread.

Once the meal was finished, instead of going to bed, the company all moved into a large living room to chat.

'Does your family always stay up this late?' she whispered to Dino.

'They are only late because they waited for us.'

As his family left the kitchen, Dino held Maria back and put an arm around her. 'They can be a little overwhelming, and you are tired, I think. Would you like to go to bed?'

'Won't that be terribly rude?'

Dino shook his head. 'They will not mind, cara. They understand we have travelled and are weary.'

He caressed her cheek, and out of the

corner of her eye Maria noticed Mrs Rossellini watching them with a smile on her face. Her own mother might disapprove of their relationship, but at least Mrs Rossellini seemed happy about it.

'I think I would prefer to go to bed.'

'That is fine.' Dino turned and spoke with his mother.

'Mamma says that you are to stay with Rob and his wife Carlotta. He only lives next door. I will take you there now.'

Dino led Maria through a connecting door in the downstairs hall and into Rob's house. He took her up many flights of narrow stairs to a small bedroom on the third floor overlooking the harbour, where her case had already been set on a chair beneath the window.

Dino pushed open the shutters for her to see the view.

The houses in the street opposite were stacked up the hill in attractive disarray, the street lights painting ribbons of gold light across the gently rippling sea in the harbour below.

'It's beautiful, Dino.' She imagined him living here as a boy, playing in the street below, messing about on the boats.

Dino stepped behind her and folded his arms protectively around her. 'I have dreamed of showing you my home, Maria. During the lonely nights away, I pictured you here with me. I told myself that if I imagined it clearly enough, it would come true ... and here you are.' He kissed her hair. 'Tomorrow we have another big family dinner in Roberto's restaurant to celebrate Mamma's birthday, but the next day my family will take Mamma out for the day to La Spezia. You and I can stay here, and I will show you round.'

* * *

The following day Maria woke late and found Dino downstairs chatting to his sister-in-law, Carlotta. They went straight up to Roberto's restaurant, the place where Rob had parked his van the night before.

The tall multi-coloured houses lined the narrow street, balconies overflowing with flowering plants in the warmth of early spring. In the daylight many of the buildings looked shabby with peeling paint, but the village was quaint and picturesque.

Dino placed a hand on Maria's back and guided her through the old wooden door of Ristorante Rossellini into a veritable treasure trove. Model boats, sea shells, and other ornaments decorated walls and shelves while nets and glass buoys dangled from the ceiling.

Three times as many people as the night before were squeezed in at the small tables dotted around the room.

'All my extended family is here today,' Dino said as he took Maria's hand and led her towards an empty table. Those already seated greeted Dino as he passed. Giuliana sat beside Maria again and while everyone else rattled away in Italian, Dino and Giuliana translated for her.

After the meal, Dino's family persuaded him to sing and his middle brother Marco joined him on the guitar. Everyone fell silent as Dino performed a medley of traditional Italian songs. Maria sipped the sweet dessert wine, sciacchetrà, a speciality of the area, while the melodious notes of Dino's voice flowed over her like a caress.

To finish, he changed tempo, making the women giggle and the men guffaw as he sang a saucy local song, which Giuliana translated with relish.

When Dino finished singing, a group of his male relatives called him over. Dino stopped behind Maria and rested his hands on her shoulders.

'Are you okay here for a little while, amore?'

'I'm fine. You go.' She smiled up at him and he kissed the top of her head.

Dino's mother came over to Maria's table with a group of women, where they dragged up more chairs and settled with cups of coffee. Giuliana introduced Dino's grandmothers, aunts and cousins. They all started talking at once, firing questions at Maria, who looked to Giuliana for a translation.

'They want to know if you and Dino have set a wedding date yet,' she said with a grin.

'Why does everyone think Dino and I are getting married?' Maria asked, embarrassed.

Giuliana shrugged. 'They are old-fashioned. If a woman is to live with a man, they believe she must be his wife — and they all love weddings, of course.'

Maria frowned, beginning to feel a little uncomfortable. 'I'm not living with Dino.'

'You will be travelling to America with him, so it comes to the same thing for them.' Giuliana gave a careless throwaway gesture. 'I told you, they are old-fashioned.'

Why did Dino's family believe she

would go to America with him? Is that what he'd told them? Is that what he expected?

★ ★ ★

Dino's family talked for hours and, although she didn't understand much, Maria frequently heard them mention Pavarotti and guessed they were discussing the film.

She had so many questions stacking up in her mind to ask Dino. She wanted some quiet time with him so that they could talk, but that didn't seem likely any time soon. His family certainly knew how to celebrate birthdays!

As darkness fell, Rob put on some recorded music. Maria sat with Giuliana, laughing while Dino tried to teach his eight-year-old niece to salsa. After they'd had still more to eat and drink, and Maria was feeling warm and tipsy, Dino pulled her up to dance with him. She'd expected to salsa, but even though the music had a lively beat,

Dino drew her into his embrace and held her close, whispering to her in Italian as they moved together.

Much later when most people had left, Dino and Maria helped Rob and Carlotta tidy up. Then they wandered back to the harbour, hand-in-hand.

Dino ambled, letting his brother and sister-in-law go on ahead. 'Did you enjoy the day, Maria?'

'It was lovely. Your family are very friendly. I just wish I could understand them.' She laughed.

'I will teach you to speak Italian. It is not so difficult.'

'Not for you!'

'I learned English.'

'I know. Your English is fantastic, but you get to practise it often. I won't get much chance to practice Italian in England.'

'Hmm.' Dino looked thoughtful as he led them past his childhood home to the edge of the harbour wall. He stared out over the gently rolling sea and sighed.

'I have to complete the rest of my concert tour. Then I should have time to spend a week with you before I travel to Hollywood to start filming.'

Maria did not want to be parted from him for so long, but the only alternative was to go with him, as his family expected, and even if she wanted to, he hadn't asked her.

'I know,' she breathed, her voice little more than a whisper.

This week in Italy was simply another oasis in the desert for them — a time when normal life stopped and they could be together for a short while. Soon Dino would be off to finish his concert tour, travelling all over Europe with Rachel Tanner. That was his real life — and not the time Maria spent with him.

'Is Rachel going with you to Hollywood?'

'No, we will not be singing together as much now I have sacked Freddy.' Dino lifted Maria's hand and kissed her palm. He looked at her from beneath his thick, dark lashes and her heart fluttered. He was so beautiful. When he could have his pick of women, she couldn't understand why he was interested in someone ordinary like her.

'I have a gift for you, my beautiful Maria.' He pulled a small jewellery box from his pocket and she pressed a hand against her mouth.

'Dino, thank you.' Maria accepted the leather box, eager to open it but also uncertain. She took her time, grabbing a few deep breaths to gain control of her racing pulse.

'You are too slow. I am impatient to see your reaction.' He laughed, low and sexy.

'I was worrying that I don't have a gift for you.'

'Having you here with me is the best gift I could ever have.'

'You have a silver tongue.'

'But it is true.' He angled his head, the moonlight glinting in his dark eyes.

Maria eased the lid up and tipped the box so that she could see the contents under a light. The gift wasn't a ring, as she had suspected, but a bracelet. Her emotions leaped and fell, then leaped again, unable to decide if she was relieved or disappointed.

Not that she had any right to expect a ring when they had known each other for such a short time, but stupidly, his relatives' insistent talk of weddings had raised her expectations.

She took out the gold bracelet and spread it on her palm. Dino relieved her of the box so that she could use both hands.

It was a charm bracelet, already full of tiny gold charms and she examined them, one by one.

'That is the Calgary coat of arms, this one is a columbine flower from Toronto — and this you must recognise.' He touched a tiny gold maple leaf. 'In every city I visited on my North American tour, I bought a charm of the city's mascot or coat of arms. You could not be with me, cara but I still wanted you to share my journey.'

For a moment, Maria couldn't speak, her chest tight with emotion. Far from forgetting all about her, Dino had thought about her in every place where he had performed.

'It's wonderful, Dino, thank you!' She rose up on tiptoe to kiss his cheek.

His arms enfolded her, capturing her against him. 'I have waited so long to give you this, amore, and there were times I feared I would never get the chance.'

He stroked her hair, kissed her temple, her cheekbone, the corner of her mouth. He brushed his lips across hers, and her eyelids fell at the blissful rush of sensation.

Maria clutched the bracelet to her heart and looped her other arm around his neck, kissing him back fervently, desperate to show him how she felt.

With every fibre of her being, she wished that Dino would give up his concerts and settle down in once place — preferably in England with her.

13

The following morning, Dino went to Rob's house and stood at the bottom of the stairs, listening for Maria. The silence suggested she was still asleep. All his family had left for La Spezia, but he had decided to stay at home so he and Maria could have some time alone together.

He trod quietly up the stairs and would have knocked on her door, but it stood ajar and he could see the bed. She lay on her side, her hair fanned across the pillow in a shiny arc.

How he longed to run his fingers through that hair, to cradle her in his arms, to kiss her, to show her how much he loved her.

He knocked softly. 'Maria, tesoro, wake up. It is nearly ten o'clock,' he whispered.

She opened her eyes and yawned.

He pushed the door a little wider and smiled. 'Downstairs I have coffee and pastries warm from Mamma's oven.'

'Mmm, I can smell them.'

She stretched out a hand to him. He slipped inside and she shuffled back so he could sit on the edge of her bed, where he gave in to his need to touch her hair, stroking it back from her face, sliding his fingers through the silky strands.

'I can't believe it's so late,' she murmured. 'Why do I sleep so long here?'

'All the sciacchetrà you drank yesterday?'

She giggled. 'That might have something to do with it.'

Dino had been so careful with Maria. Not that he was one to jump in bed with a woman as soon as he met her, but he was not usually this restrained. Maria was too important to him to rush things. Yet sitting on her bed while she lay warm and beautifully sleepy beside him, he wanted desperately to climb in with her. She filled his dreams, starred in his fantasies. His need for her had crept up on him when he wasn't looking and taken him over and she probably had no idea what a powerful effect she had on him.

He stroked a finger along her cheekbone, brushed the corner of her mouth. She stilled, her eyes on him; her pupils large and dark in the blue-grey of her irises.

One day she would be his, and when she was, he would bring her pleasure. One day soon, when his few remaining concerts were over. He planned to take her to America with him when he started filming. He would not be without her again.

He stood and smiled as she stretched. 'I will be downstairs, cara, but do not keep me waiting too long or I will eat all the pastries myself.'

★　★　★

With a little sigh of longing, Maria watched Dino slip out the door. He wore faded jeans with worn holes in the knees, and a checked shirt. It was the first time she had seen him out of smart clothes, but he still looked just as gorgeous.

She touched the corner of her lips where his finger had been and wished he had kissed her. Italians were known to be amorous, but Dino certainly wasn't so with her, despite the long list of women he was supposed to have dated.

Maria pushed away her insecurities, had a quick shower and hurried downstairs, her nose following the delicious fragrance of the pastries.

After breakfast, Dino showed her round Riomaggiore. It might be a seaside fishing village like Porthale, but there the similarity ended. The village was crammed into a narrow valley, the tall houses perched almost one atop the other up the steep hills on either side. Because of the geography, there was only one main street and few vehicles. Most of the houses could only be reached by foot, following narrow walkways that twisted and turned. Maria had never mounted so many steps. Although she considered herself to be fit, her legs ached, and she was soon out of breath.

Every corner revealed a new delight. Potted plants adorned nooks and ledges, adding welcome splashes of colour. She took off her coat and carried it, the sleeves of her blouse pushed up to the elbows. By midday, the temperature was as warm as a British summer's day.

The place was a wonderland of curiosities. Tiny windows and crooked stairs, old metal gates up narrow side alleys, overgrown and mysterious.

'I wish I had my camera to take photos to show my family,' she said ruefully when they reached a viewpoint outside a church. In the rush to leave home she had forgotten it. She stared out over the higgledy-piggledy roofs at the sparkling water in the bay below.

Dino put his arm around her. 'Bring

your camera on your next visit. Now I show you where I played as a boy.'

He took her to a tiny house with paint peeling from the walls. Dino smiled wistfully.

'My best friend Romeo lived here with his nonna, his grandmother. He and I would ride down the streets on a wooden cart we made from driftwood and crash into the walls! Mamma did not approve of Romeo, but he charmed her with his smile — as he did all the girls.'

They walked down the grey paved main street, mingling with the locals and a few early tourists and Maria browsed the windows of gift shops.

Dino led her past the houses, up a steep path and out onto the rocks. They stood high on a cliff looking down at the sea, and Dino held her hand tightly.

'Romeo and I stood here and shouted our dreams to the wind.' He laughed. 'We would spread our arms like wings and try to fly, but when we jumped off we always fell into the sea.'

'Goodness!' Maria leaned out and peered over at the white-capped waves rolling against the cliffs. 'You were either very brave or a little mad.'

'Back then, Romeo and I thought we were invincible, cara.'

He led her back towards the houses and along a path by the edge of the sea. They passed through a metal gateway with two entwined hearts above.

'Now we will walk the Via dell, amore — Lovers' Lane.'

It looked like a coast path to Maria — a very smart paved coast path, but still just a path beside the sea.

They strolled arm in arm. The views were fantastic, the steep rocky cliffs hollowed out by a succession of small coves. Above them the cliff was home to plants and flowers while at the top she caught glimpses of vineyards and olive orchards. The soothing sound of the sea accompanied them, reminding Maria again of home.

After a while they came to a place where the path cut through the cliff face. One wall was decorated with romantic graffiti, heartfelt words left by decades of lovers. On the other side, the Mediterranean was visible through arches cut in the rock.

Dino smiled and pointed at a strange sight. In the centre of one of the arches was a statue of a kissing couple with a bench below. On either side, the railings were adorned with padlocks of various shapes and sizes.

'What on earth is that about?' Maria asked.

'The padlocks symbolise eternal love and commitment. Boys and girls from Riomaggiore and the next village, Manarola, have met here for decades. Couples come to attach padlocks to show their love is forever.'

He drew a brass padlock from his jacket pocket with their names engraved on it and Maria gave a soft gasp as she realised the significance.

'Maria, amore mio.' He drew her down on the loveseat beside him. 'I know I did not start this well, walking out and leaving you without a goodbye, but please believe that you mean everything to me. To prove this, I attach this padlock here.' He snapped the metal device in amongst the mass of others and tossed the key into the sea. 'Now our love is locked in forever and can never be undone.'

Oblivious to the other people walking past, Dino pulled her onto his lap and kissed her. Then he pressed his lips to her ear and whispered, 'I love you, Maria. Will you marry me?'

Warm and languorous in his arms, it took Maria a moment for his words to register before the joy filled her in an overwhelming wave. He loved her! Then the rest of what he'd said sank in.

She trembled inside with a potent mix of excitement and trepidation. She loved Dino and wanted to be with him more than anything else in the world — but if she married him he would expect her to follow him wherever he went.

'I thought you had to go away again?'

'I do, but only for a few weeks until I finish my concert tour. If we get engaged now, our families can organise the wedding and you can come to America with me as my wife. I do not want to be parted from you for months and months while I am filming, amore. Please, say yes.'

On a hollow pulse of panic she remembered her dreadful time in Canada with Tom and the unsuccessful trip to New York.

'Where will we live? Will I be able to come to work with you while you're filming?'

'Do not worry about the details, cara. We will be able to work everything out later.'

But Maria needed to know the details. All the blood seemed to drain out of her head and she heard her pulse beating in her ears. She didn't want to be left on her own all day while Dino was busy, with no friends or family to depend on.

'But what happens if I don't like it,

Dino?' If they were married she could hardly come home without him if she were unhappy while abroad.

Dino's hopeful expression faded and tiny lines appeared between his beautiful dark eyebrows.

'Maria, what is the matter?'

'I love you, Dino.' She kissed him to prove the point — the last thing she wanted was to hurt his feelings. 'And I really do want to marry you and spend my life with you, but . . . '

He cupped her cheek in his palm and examined her face. 'But you are not happy about travelling, is that it?'

She nodded.

He pulled her close again and pressed his lips to her hair, rocking her as if she were a frightened child.

'You are the most precious thing in my life,' he whispered, his breath warm against her skin. 'If it distresses you to travel, then I will give up the film. For you I will settle in England. Trust me, amore, your happiness comes first to me and I will do whatever I must to take care of you.'

Relief rushed through her. 'Thank you, Dino, thank you!'

She framed his face between her hands and kissed him again. He was so kind and thoughtful; she should have known he would put her feelings first.

Dino lifted her off his lap and settled her by his side, then he dug in his pocket and pulled out a ring.

'Before Mamma left for La Spezia I told her I would ask you to marry me. She gave me this ring. It was her grandmother's and she wants you to have it, but if you want a new ring, cara, then tell me.'

He held out a beautiful gold ring with a square-cut emerald flanked by four diamonds.

'It's lovely, Dino. How sweet of your mum. This is perfect.'

He slipped it on her ring finger and kissed her hand.

'It fits so well. It was meant for you, I think.' He hugged her tightly. 'I am afraid Mamma cannot keep a secret.

My family, they will all be waiting to celebrate with us.'

'What would you have done if I'd said no?'

'No woman could turn down such an opportunity.' He attempted an arrogant lift of his eyebrows but spoiled it by grinning broadly.

Maria giggled, her heart so light with happiness that she was sure if she jumped off Dino's cliff right now, the wind would carry her up with his dreams.

Dino stood and pulled her to her feet. 'Come, let us go and share our good news and drink lots of Roberto's expensive champagne.'

Gripping Dino's hand, Maria hugged his side as they wandered back along the coast path. He stopped to kiss her and they chatted and laughed.

Inside, Maria trembled with joy and anticipation. A few weeks ago it had seemed as though her dreams were dead, but now they were all coming true. Dino had agreed to settle in

England! Now she just had to persuade him to buy a guesthouse similar to the Crow's Nest for her to run; somewhere happy to raise their children. Life would be perfect with Dino at her side.

When they arrived back at the harbour, Dino's family were waiting for them outside, enjoying the sun, the men leaning against the wall chatting, while Carlotta and Giuliana played with the children.

Giuliana leaped to her feet the moment she saw Dino and Maria and skipped towards them, grinning.

'You said yes? Please say you said yes?'

'I said yes.'

Giuliana squealed and grabbed Maria's hand to examine the ring. 'This is so wonderful! I have another sister! Tonight we will get drunk and celebrate.'

'Not too much drinking,' Dino said, dropping a kiss on his sister's forehead. 'Maria has to fly home tomorrow. She doesn't want a headache.'

'Spoilsport!' Giuliana batted Dino's shoulder and grabbed Maria's arm. 'Come and see Mamma.'

Maria was congratulated by the gaggle of women who crowded around her to see the ring while Dino's brothers slapped him on the back and hugged him.

Mrs Rossellini appeared in the doorway and opened her arms to Maria. She allowed herself to be drawn into a warm hug. Dino's mother spoke to her in Italian, tears shining in her eyes, and Giuliana translated. 'Mamma says she is delighted to welcome you into our family and she knows you will take good care of her little boy and make him happy.'

'Thank you. I will certainly do my best.'

It was funny how that had been her first inclination when Dino arrived at the Crow's Nest — to take care of him and make him happy. Although back then, she had never dreamed that she would be doing it for the rest of her life.

She smiled to herself, remembering how much Dino enjoyed her cooking, and how she loved looking after him.

But as Rob popped the cork on a bottle of champagne and sloshed bubby into her glass an unsettling question crept into her mind. Would Dino really be happy living in a guesthouse? After all, that wasn't his dream, but hers.

A trail of excited boys and girls scooted around her legs and she laughed, letting her doubts slip away. Maria couldn't wait to have children and she was certain that Dino would make a wonderful father.

Dino came to her side, slipped an arm around her waist and kissed her. 'My family are so happy, amore. They already love you as much as I do. Now you will have to learn Italian so you can talk to your mother-in-law.' He tapped the end of her nose and she giggled, light headed from happiness and champagne.

'I must call Mum and Dad and tell them the good news.'

With a smile, Maria wandered away from the merry group, pulled her mobile phone from her pocket and dialled. It was Chris who answered.

'Oh, Mari, that's fantastic news!' Chris burst out the moment Maria mentioned marriage. 'I know you'll be happy. Dino is such a great guy — and so smokin' hot. Tina will be jealous. I'm jealous! You will make beautiful babies.'

'I hope so.'

'Oh, goodness, you'll get to go to Hollywood with him!' Chris gave a little squeal. 'You lucky, lucky thing.'

For some reason Maria stumbled over her response. 'Um . . . I . . . I don't think that's going to happen now.'

'Oh, no! Why? Did the movie people drop him? Poor Dino! He was so excited about the film. He must be devastated.'

Maria swallowed, taken aback by Chris's reaction. She ought to explain that it was Dino's decision, he hadn't been dropped, but it was difficult to describe the reason over the phone.

'Can I speak to Mum?'

A moment later, her mother came on the line.

'I'm so happy for you, darling,' she said and Maria heard the smile in her voice. 'I was obviously wrong about him.'

Her mother's approval lifted a huge weight off her shoulders.

'I do love him, Mum. I know you were worried, but he's willing to make changes in his life so I'm happy.'

Maria discussed her plans for the next few weeks, then her mum passed the phone back to Chris.

'Drink lots of champagne, enjoy your yummy Italian, then come home and give me all the juicy details.' Chris giggled. 'Oh, and remember to tell Dino that I'm really sorry the film fell through, but he's so talented and gorgeous he's bound to be asked to star in something even better. See you tomorrow.'

Maria dropped her phone back in her pocket and bit her lip. She was relieved by her mum's reaction to her news, but unsettled by the way Chris made such a big deal about Dino pulling out of the film.

She glanced back at the happy family group celebrating in the sun and even the neighbours who had come out to congratulate Dino. He chatted and laughed, sipping champagne.

What would his family say when they found out he was backing out of the Pavarotti film? It had been one of the main topics of conversation. All his relatives had sounded excited and whenever Dino spoke about the film he had positively glowed with enthusiasm.

* * *

Maria slept badly that night. She tossed and turned, Chris's words plaguing her like ants under her skin. She woke at dawn to the sound of men talking outside and lay in the semi-darkness listening to the musical lilt of the beautiful Italian voices.

When she realised sleep had fled, she climbed from bed and pulled open the shutters. Dino's brother Marco was underneath her window preparing one of the boats for launching. He looked so much like Dino, even had the same mannerisms.

If Dino had not been determined to sing, this would have been his life and she would never have met him.

Her gaze was drawn up the hill to what she thought of as Dino's cliff. At the sight of a lone figure striding up the coast path, her breath caught with a sense of déjà vu. Even from this distance she recognised Dino. He halted in the spot where he had jumped into the sea with his friend as a boy, and stared into the distance.

Maria clutched the edges of the shutters. What was Dino doing, walking alone this early? Was something troubling him?

She dressed quickly, only stopping to brush her teeth and run a comb through her hair before slipping quietly downstairs and out of the front door. Marco had his back to her as she darted past and hurried up the cliff path, her heart pounding as much with worry as from the incline.

By the time she approached Dino the sun was higher, gleaming off his black hair as if each strand was polished. Her breath caught as she stared at his darkly handsome profile, but her heart pinched.

Dino was so still, his gaze fixed in the distance. His usual aura of energy and enthusiasm was strangely muted. Was he having second thoughts about their marriage?

'Dino,' she said tentatively. Uncertainty flashed through her when, lost in his thoughts, he didn't respond. He was normally so vital and attentive. She hadn't seen him like this since he first arrived in Cornwall. For some reason, he was hurting. She ached inside at the thought that it might be because of her.

'Dino,' Maria repeated, moving closer so that he had to notice her.

His head whipped around, startled, and for an instant she caught the sadness in his eyes before he smiled.

'Maria, what are you doing up so early?' He extended his arm and she went to him. His large warm hand engulfed hers and he lifted it to his lips and kissed her fingers.

'Voices outside woke me. Then I looked up here and saw you . . . ' she said tentatively.

He turned back to stare out to sea. 'I needed some time alone before I leave.'

Maria leaned against Dino's side and he wrapped his arm around her waist. 'What are you thinking?' she asked.

'Ah — now that we are engaged you want to know all my secrets, do you, cara?' He flashed her a wry smile.

'Not if you don't want to tell me.'

He sucked in a breath then raised his hand and opened his fingers as if releasing something fragile into the wind. He whispered some words in Italian and then fell silent for a few moments. 'There, it is done.'

'What is?'

'I have let go of my childhood dreams. Now I dream only of being with you, cara, of our life together.' He turned to smile at her, but a hint of sadness still lingered around his eyes and tore at her heart.

'You don't need to forget your dreams, Dino.'

'But I do, amore. I have chosen to be with you instead.'

'I don't expect you to give up everything you've worked so hard for.' Even as the words left her mouth, she knew she'd lied; this was exactly what she'd asked of him. If he gave up travelling and lived in England, it was impossible for his career to thrive and grow.

The first time she saw him, saw the hollow sadness in his eyes, she had promised herself she would make him feel better, take care of him, but somewhere along the way she had forgotten that promise, forgotten Dino's feelings.

A rush of shame raised goose bumps on Maria's arms. Whenever she considered Dino's career, she thought of it as a nuisance that hindered them being together; it interfered with her vision of the life she wanted. She had only paid lip service to the fact that, by singing, he was fulfilling his dreams.

She stared over the rocky cliff where Dino had risked life and limb trying to fly, and realised that daring little boy had succeeded. He had flown up among the stars, to the peak of his profession, achieved what few men ever would.

Yet he was willing to give it up for her.

'I don't know what I've done to deserve you,' she said, remorse tightening her throat. She loved him, she wanted him to be happy, to have the rewards he'd worked so hard for.

His arm tightened around her. 'You only need to be yourself, amore, that is enough.'

But she knew it wasn't nearly

enough. If she clipped his wings, she didn't deserve his love and devotion.

'Dino, is playing Pavarotti really such a big honour?'

His gaze grew unfocused, a hint of longing on his face. 'I would lie if I said otherwise. It is a tenor's dream to be chosen to portray such an icon.'

'I want you to do this film, Dino. If it's this big a deal, you can't give it up for me.'

He stepped back from the cliff, turned to face her. 'No. I will not leave you behind again.'

'Then I'll come with you, darling Dino.'

'You will? You do not mind coming with me?'

In that moment she realised it was true; she didn't mind taking a chance — not if she had Dino by her side.

She had been hanging on to the past for too long. No wonder her mum had been overprotective of her when she had clung to home like a child.

She stepped towards him, gazing into

his eyes. 'As long as I'm with you, that's all that matters, Dino. I love you.'

'Ah, Maria, your words make my heart sing!' He pulled her close and kissed her so softly and tenderly that it brought tears to her eyes.

She needn't be frightened of travelling, not with Dino. He loved her, and she trusted him to be there when she needed him. Wherever they went in the world, she knew that she would always be safe in his arms.

THE END

THE TEMP AND THE TYCOON

Liz Fielding

Talie Calhoun had briefly met billionaire Jude Radcliffe whilst working as a temp at the Radcliffe Group. It was a rare holiday away from nursing her invalid mother. But when she's asked to accompany Mr Radcliffe to New York, she is over the moon. However, Radcliffe is furious with his secretary's choice of temp. But Talie is a vibrant woman and, as he becomes drawn to her, Jude becomes determined to take care of her and make her his own.

LOVE TRIUMPHANT

Margaret Mounsdon

Steve Baxter disappears while interior designer Lizzie Hilton is working on the refurbishment of his property. His brother, Todd, suspects Lizzie of becoming romantically involved with Steve, knowing that he is due to come into an inheritance upon marriage. Lizzie challenges Todd to find evidence to substantiate his outrageous allegation. But when Paul Owen appears on the scene Lizzie panics — because Paul can provide Todd with the evidence he is looking for . . .